Prol

October 15, 2005 East St. Louis, IL

Landon's surroundings were all too familiar. The dark bedroom with the fan going overhead, the smell of sweat and sex filling the air, and a warm body lying next to him. At least this one he knew. The woman lying next to him was his first, but certainly not his last.

He sighed. He'd come to her because it was his birthday weekend. Eighteen years in this life and heartbroken, he'd gone back for one more round with someone that cared about him. He wanted to forget his recent heartbreak. His first venture in love with a man in this life hadn't gone well at all. Most things in his life didn't go well, not now that he knew who and what he was. So, he'd gone to what he knew before the truth was revealed.

What a truth it was. He wasn't even human. No wonder his life was in shambles. He had lived this life only as a punishment from his king. He didn't fit in here because he was ruled by his emotions. He felt things far more strongly than a human. He was a Magus, a race of nigh immortal and powerful beings who had been many things across the span of time. The knowledge of what he was and what he was capable of was starting to overwhelm him. As he looked at his reflection in the mirror across the room, he could see certain changes in himself. Sure, he was still a light brown skinned skinny Black guy with long deep brown, almost black hair and brown eyes. But he was a

1

guy who had never worked out a day in his life and he had a six-pack coming in. His eyes were a bit lighter than they'd been before and damned if his hair didn't seem to have a new sheen to it.

The woman stirred beside him, and he watched as she stretched before looking up at him.

"How long was I out?" she asked.

"About an hour or so, I guess," he answered dully.

"What's with you?" she asked.

He looked down at her. "Sorry, I've got a lot on my mind."

She chuckled. "I figured as much if you're here."

Landon studied her, debating on whether to ask his next question.

"What is it?"

He sighed and went ahead with his question. "Are you even single anymore?"

She made no reply.

"Shell," he said sternly, demanding a response.

"No, I'm not, but since when does that matter?" she snapped back.

"Who is he?" he questioned, a sinking feeling in his stomach.

He watched as she bit her lower lip. She was debating on whether to tell him the truth. He could sense it. If he wanted, he could force the truth out of her or find it himself, but he hated to do it. Instead, he'd let her tell him on her own. While he waited, he looked over her nude body. She was a slender young woman with a curvy figure he enjoyed far too much for his own good and decent sized breasts that he'd explored

Shadows of the Past

Journeys, Volume 1

Drako

Published by Drako, 2024.

This is a work of fiction. Similarities to real people, places, or events are entirely coincidental.

SHADOWS OF THE PAST

First edition. May 20, 2024.

Copyright © 2024 Drako.

ISBN: 979-8224447732

Written by Drako.

Table of Contents

thoroughly in the last several hours. She rolled onto her stomach, giving him a view of her ample backside.

Finally, she decided to answer him. "His name is Josh."

"As in my old friend, Josh?" he asked, even though he knew the answer.

"Yeah, that Josh," she responded quietly.

"You do realize the mess this is going to cause, right?" Landon sighed again. "Don't you think you should have turned me down?"

Shell rolled her eyes. "Why would I do that?"

Landon scowled even though she couldn't see it in the dark. "Do you know what it means to be faithful? If I'd known, then this wouldn't have happened. I can do without birthday sex, believe it or not."

She sat up and turned on a light to glare at him. "You and I both know that's exactly why you didn't ask me before. You wanted this and you didn't want any reason not to do it."

Landon stood and began dressing again. "The last thing I need is the drama he would bring. If he catches me here, he'll know what it means. I'd rather not have to hurt your boyfriend."

Shell made a noise of frustration as she got up and got dressed as well. Once they were dressed, they left her apartment. Sadly, a quick escape was not in the cards. As soon as they were out of the door, they ran into the very person they were hoping to avoid.

"Ah, fuck," Landon muttered.

Josh looked back and forth between the two. "So, that's how it is, huh?"

Shell quickly moved towards him. "Calm down, Josh. I can explain."

"Explain?" Josh laughed bitterly. "Explain why the fuck your ex-boyfriend is here. Go ahead, I'm dying to know. Please tell me why someone you clearly never got over is here."

"Well, this is bound to be fun," Landon mumbled, shaking his head.

"Look, it just happened, alright? Lose the attitude."

This bitch can't be this stupid, Landon thought.

"Lose the attitude?!" Josh was actually flabbergasted. "You're cheating on me, with him of all people! He doesn't even live near here. That shit didn't just happen. You planned it!"

Landon tuned them out. The argument was pointless. Josh was right. This had been planned. After all, Landon lived in St. Louis, Missouri. Belleville, Illinois was not his neck of the woods. Frankly, he would never come over here if not for her. His attention was brought back to the argument as he noticed Josh push Shell aside and come for him.

"You really do not want to go down this road right now," he warned.

"Do I look scared to you, you scrawny little fuck?" Josh took the first swing.

Landon ducked under him and punched him in the stomach. The force knocked the wind from the other, larger male and Landon punched him right in the face with all the force he could muster. Josh hit the ground and Landon mounted him, raining down blow after blow on the other male. He didn't care where he hit him, as long as he hit him. He had so much rage pent up inside and Josh was the perfect target for

4

him. But his wailing away on the guy was cut short when Shell grabbed his arm.

"That's enough, stop hitting him!" She pulled his arm until he rose off of the other man.

"He came at me first." Landon snatched his arm away. "I told you this would be a problem."

Josh sat up and spat out some of the blood pooling in his mouth. "We're not done! You think you can just come back and fuck my girl behind my back with no consequences?!"

"First off, I didn't realize she was your girl. Frankly, I didn't give a shit. Not my fault she still wants what I got," Landon shot back.

"Oh, you son of a bitch!" Josh launched himself at Landon, tackling him to the ground. This time, he was in the mounted position, attempting to wail away at him.

Landon grabbed his fist and pulled him down just enough to head-butt him in the face. Josh's nose broke and gushed blood as he fell back. He got up and ran off, his hand over his nose.

"That was too damn easy." Landon brushed himself off and looked at Shell. "Go inside, now."

"But..." she started to argue.

"Do what I say!" he growled.

She ran away. Landon went after Josh, who had reached his car and went into the trunk.

"Fuck my life," he muttered.

He knew Josh and what he kept on him. How the hell the guy got his hands on a gun was beyond Landon, but he didn't have time to debate it. The human was going to go down today. Coming around to the other man's car, he clocked him right in the jaw as he finished loading his piece. The gun hit the ground before Landon could see what it was exactly. He didn't care. Planting his fist wherever he could was far more important.

"I'm getting real sick of your shit." Landon punched him in the side. "If you're going to start a fight, don't bitch out when you get your ass kicked." He punched him in the jaw, knocking him to the ground. "Punk bitch."

Josh curled up after Landon kicked him hard in the stomach. He coughed up more blood. His lip was busted but he was pretty sure some of it came from inside him as well. Landon hit hard for such a skinny guy, but then again, Landon wasn't exactly a normal guy.

Landon stood over him, waiting for him to move again. "I swear to God, I will fucking end you right here. Don't fucking test me. Get the fuck up and get in your car. Drive away and rethink this shit. Or swing again and get fucked up."

Josh pushed himself up again. "Fuck you! I'm sick of always being in your shadow. You were her first and she always comes back to you!"

"Once mine, always mine, bitch," Landon sneered.

"She's supposed to be *mine*. You fuck guys, remember?"

Landon rolled his eyes. "Yeah, and I fuck girls too. Whichever suits my mood. Don't start shit with me because you can't put it on her right."

Josh growled and launched himself at him again. Landon swore as he hit the ground, this time on concrete. Josh got a few good shots in this time, splitting Landon's lip. Landon managed to shove him off and got back to his feet, instantly going for the knife he kept on him at all times. Flicking the blade open, he threw it with surprisingly good aim. Josh had gotten to his gun and fired a shot. Neither found their intended mark.

Shell had run back outside and neither of the two of them had seen her during their scuffle. They watched in horror as her shirt was stained crimson and she dropped to the ground.

Landon kneeled down next to her first. His knife had embedded in her back. It wasn't the kill shot. He knew the kill shot had been the literal shot from Josh. Josh kneeled across from him, blubbering. Shell looked at Landon. Her life was fading quickly, but she mouthed something to him. Landon understood and nodded. Across from him, Josh was in a panic.

"Shut up!" Landon slapped him. "You're the one waving around a damn gun. Now fucking deal with the consequences."

"We're going to jail, man. We're murderers. And worst of all, we murdered the woman we love."

Landon fought not to roll his eyes. He'd rather not have an idiot speak for him.

"Look, she's gone. I can't change that and I don't have time to dwell on it. If you want to keep your ass out of jail, do exactly as I say. And never, ever breathe a word of this to anyone." Landon grabbed his face to force eye contact. "Shut the fuck up and nod your head yes before I knock it off your shoulders."

Josh nodded. "What do I need to do?"

"Start by shutting the fuck up. I can't stress that enough. Then, give me the gun. I'll handle the rest."

Landon looked down into Shell's lifeless eyes. He closed them and sighed. Those eyes would always haunt him. A nagging voice in the back of his mind chastised him for giving in to his base emotions stemming from this forced life as a human. Deep down, he knew that this was his fault. He'd asked no questions and taken what he wanted. When confronted, he'd used it as an excuse to engage in violence. Truth be told, if he'd been at full strength, it wouldn't have gone on so long. One well placed hit would have killed Josh. He knew better than to engage this way. This death was on him, not Josh. As he stood up, a green light flashed across his eyes. He would have to solve this the Magus way and learn from his mistake.

Chapter One

July 2010

Landon found himself at the Metrolink Station, the local public transit train. He was there to catch the train downtown rather than drive or just will himself there. There were some drawbacks to being in the mortal world, after all. While he could will himself anywhere he wanted to, explaining that to mortals was more hassle than it was worth. Besides, travelling could be fun.

He was dressed simply in blue jeans, white Nikes, and a black t-shirt with a large gold dragon design. It was a warm July day and he was comfortable. Going to the platform, he flashed his pass at the security guard and went on to take a seat at the end in the shade. He was waiting for the train, as well as his friend. Scanning the crowd, he spotted a redhead rushing towards the platform.

Landon smiled. That was Renee, his best friend. She was dressed in blue jeans and a red halter top, her long fire engine red hair flowing behind her. She had smooth sun-tanned skin and bright green eyes, which flashed happily as she spotted him. Landon stood as she reached him and caught her in a hug. She was a few inches shorter than him and slimmer, but with a feminine, curvy figure. Not really top heavy either, but to Landon she was absolutely gorgeous, for a human anyway.

"Sorry I'm late," she told him.

"It's cool. I haven't been here long," Landon replied.

"When does the next train come?"

Landon shrugged. "I didn't check the schedule."

The two sat down on the bench.

"So, where are we heading today?" Renee asked.

"Laclede's Landing," Landon answered. "It's just a hangout day."

"Hmm, where's Kevin?'

Landon shrugged. "He said he'd meet up with me later."

Renee studied him. "You don't seem pleased with that."

Landon snorted. "I'm not. I'm trying to be patient with him but it's aggravating. We don't go anywhere together anymore."

Renee hooked her arm through his. "I'm sure he'll come around. You have to remember you're his first. He's probably going to take a long time to be comfortable with this lifestyle."

Landon didn't respond. Kevin was Landon's boyfriend. Prior to Landon, Kevin had only been with women. They'd been friends working together at their first job at a local Sonic Drive-In, and had gotten close as Landon revealed the problems he'd had with the men he'd dated. Since making the transition from friends to lovers, the two only met at Landon's apartment and never went out together. Kevin had naturally chosen to be a closet case.

The train pulled up and Landon and Renee got on and took a seat together.

"It's been six months, Renee," Landon commented. "Six months of only late night visits. I'm not asking for him to hold my hand or kiss me in public. I just want him to make a step towards showing me I'm not wasting my time. I'm beginning to feel like a sideline, which means he has a main one at home. I haven't been to his new apartment."

"You should talk to him about it," Renee told him.

"I have talked to him. He just keeps changing the subject." Landon sighed. "It's so frustrating. I'm torn between staying and leaving him."

"Well in the end, you have to do what's best for you. Do you think he wants to be open with your relationship, or is he content with the way things are? And can you continue to live like this, or do you need to have someone comfortable with who they are?"

Landon thought for a few seconds. "I've been thinking that maybe this is all he wants, and no, I can't continue on like this. But at the moment, I can't bring myself to let go."

Renee laid her head on his shoulder. "I'm sorry. But this is the drawback to turning out a straight guy."

Landon scowled. "It's not like I intended to turn him out. We were just friends at work. It's not my fault after we got to know each other he caught feelings."

"It's totally your fault for having such a magnetic personality."

Landon laughed. "Magnetic personality?"

Renee smiled up at him. "You're a bit rough around the edges, but that's what he likes. You're not a flamboyant, blatantly obvious queen. You're a normal guy who happens to be gay. You're just like one of the boys."

"Yeah, except I'm confined to my apartment with him," Landon muttered.

There was no way to get around that. The two reached their stop and got off the train, heading out of the station and to the park with the famous Gateway Arch. They walked arm in arm, a natural habit for them.

11

"So, how's life with you these days?" Landon asked.

"I'm single and loving it personally," Renee replied. "I just don't have time for men. I'm content with being alone."

Again, Landon had no response. Perhaps he should venture back into single life again. He didn't really want to, but maybe it was what he needed.

His thoughts were interrupted as his phone went off, alerting him to a text message. He pulled out his phone to check it.

Hey babe. Where r u?

It was Kevin. Landon sighed as he responded.

At the Landing with Renee. Told you where I was going

Renee looked at his phone as he sent the reply. "If he's smart, he'll figure out you're mad."

"I'm not mad, just tired," Landon responded.

Renee rolled her eyes. "Which makes you mad. I know you all too well. The frown on your face tells it all."

Landon hadn't even noticed he was frowning, and it didn't go away as he received Kevin's next text.

My bad, I forgot. How long you gonna be?

Renee laughed. "Wow, he's stupid."

"The spelling in his texts didn't give it away?" Landon asked bitterly as he typed out his reply.

I don't know. We just got here and we're not in a hurry.

"Surely he'll get it now," Renee commented.

"I doubt it," Landon replied.

Another text came in.

What's wrong with u?

"Ha! I was right!" Renee exclaimed.

Landon rolled his eyes as he responded.

SHADOWS OF THE PAST

You already know the answer

"He's a guy, sweetie," Renee told him. "He probably has no clue."

"Then I guess he'll have to figure it out," Landon replied.

Another text came through.

Answer the dam question cuz I don't know

Renee laughed and Landon ignored her as he responded. Mortal men were so damn frustrating.

I tried talking to you about it. You didn't want to hear it.

Renee and Landon sat on a bench next to the arch, and another text came in.

Ok let's talk about it tonight

Renee just watched as Landon replied.

I might be out late. Maybe tomorrow

"Nice," Renee told him.

"I'm tired of being on his schedule."

And in came Kevin's reply.

So I can't come thru?

Landon smirked as he typed in his reply.

Nope

"Are you sure about that?" Renee asked.

"I'm positive. It's time to get serious." Landon stood up. "Now, let's go get food."

Chapter Two

Landon and Renee had just finished eating when another text came through.

Come to the Metrolink

Landon raised an eyebrow and responded. *Why?*

"What did he say?" Renee asked.

"He told me to come to the Metrolink," Landon answered.

Renee laughed. "This is going to be hilarious. He actually came down here?"

Landon frowned as he read the next text.

Just bring yo ass

Renee looked over and read the text, then laughed again. "He's a demanding little fucker isn't he?'

Landon ignored her as he replied. *I'll be there in a few.*

Landon gave his debit card to the waiter to pay for their meal. One of the few things he found convenient in this world was the way in which they stored their money.

"This is funny to me," Renee commented.

"What are you talking about?" Landon asked irritably.

"Your situation," she answered. "And the way he talks. Since when do you allow that?"

"Apparently DL guys making their first venture into gay life are more aggressive. And we were this way before when we were just friends."

The waiter returned with his card and receipt as another text came through.

SHADOWS OF THE PAST

Don't make me come look 4 u

Landon signed the receipt before sending his response. *Fuck you. I said I'd be there in a few.*

He stood up afterwards and Renee followed suit. They walked up the street to the Metrolink station, where Kevin stood at the entrance. He was taller than Landon by a couple of inches and not as slim. He had dark chocolate skin and dark brown eyes. Unlike Landon he kept a low cut and was dressed in black baggy jeans and black wife beater, showing off well defined arms and pecs. Around his neck was a long gold chain with a dragon at the end. He stood looking at his phone and biting his lower lip, a nervous habit of his that Landon normally found adorable. At that moment, it irritated him beyond belief.

"You rang?" He questioned as they stopped in front of Kevin.

Kevin frowned at the tone in his voice. "I came to hang out with you."

Landon folded his arms across his chest. "Oh really?"

Kevin sighed. "Babe, I'm trying. This is hard for me."

"Dude, we hung out before. It shouldn't be any different now."

Renee placed a hand on Landon's shoulder. "Hey, this shows progress. Let's go enjoy ourselves."

Landon sighed, relenting. "Yeah, you're right." He looked at Kevin. "I'm sorry."

"It's cool. I know this is hard on you."

Renee stepped between the two and hooked one arm in each of theirs. "Now I've got two men for today."

"Such a hoe," Landon joked.

"Oh no, I'm clearly the pimp and you're my hoes," Renee replied.

Kevin laughed. "You two are weird."

"Normal is boring," Renee told him as she led them off into the park.

When night fell, the trio finally got back on the train to head towards home. In the rows of two seats, Kevin actually sat next to Landon, while Renee sat in the row behind them. Landon took the window seat and stared out at the passing scenery while Kevin stared at him. Finally, Kevin leaned in closer to be heard over the sound of the train.

"You know, I had fun today," he commented.

"Mmhmm," was all Landon said in response.

"We really need to talk, and don't tell me not tonight."

"You're not just going to want to talk." Landon looked at him. "You might let the conversation start, but then you won't want to hear it. Which leads to you wanting sex, which leads to sex, which leads to a shower and sleep. And in the end, nothing was solved."

"No, I'm not going to be that way. We really need to talk about this. It's bothering you too much."

Landon knew he wouldn't win this so he relented. "Fine, you can come to the house and we'll try again."

"Don't sound like that. I mean it."

"We'll see, Kevin, we'll see."

Kevin placed a hand on his knee, and Landon forced himself not to react. The rest of the ride was spent in silence. Once they got back to Hanley Station, the three got off the train together and walked off the platform.

"Well, guys, it's been fun but I'm heading home." Renee looked at both of them. "Tomorrow we should do dinner at my house."

"I'd like that," Kevin said as he looked at Landon for confirmation.

Landon shrugged. "I'll let you know."

Renee hugged them both and walked off to her car. Kevin turned back to Landon.

"Mind if I ride with you?" he asked. "I didn't drive."

Landon nodded and led the way to his car. Once inside, he started it and pulled off, heading towards his apartment.

"Hold on, babe, go to my house," Kevin told him.

"You sure?" Landon asked.

"Yeah, I don't have any clothes at your house."

"Oh." Landon found it hard to hide his disappointment.

"What's wrong?" Kevin asked.

"Nothing," Landon lied.

"You're lying."

"Blow me."

Kevin smirked. "Gladly, but that'll have to wait. Something else is bothering you."

"It's nothing I can't deal with."

"You don't have to deal with it. Just tell me and I'll try to fix it."

Landon snorted. "Yeah right."

Kevin frowned. "You know me. I don't just say shit I don't mean."

Landon gave him a brief, bland stare before refocusing on the road.

"What was that for?" Kevin asked.

DRAKO

"I've known you for seven years. I know how you were with women, and that makes your last statement a lie." Landon pulled into the Springwood Apartments complex where Kevin lived. Driving around to the back of the complex he pulled into a parking space and turned the car off. Kevin got out and Landon merely sat in the car to wait. Kevin stopped and stuck his head in.

"Come on."

"Aren't you just getting clothes?" Landon asked.

"Get your ass out of the car," Kevin demanded before closing the door.

Landon got out and locked the door before following Kevin to his apartment. Kevin had a corner apartment in the two-story building, on the bottom floor right next to the stairs. Coming in, they entered the living room, which had only a futon and a TV on a stand in it. On the stand were a PS3 and several games. There was a breakfast bar separating the kitchen from the living room and off to the right of the kitchen were the bathroom and bedroom, which he couldn't see currently. Landon took a seat on the futon and Kevin sat next to him, quickly pulling him close and wrapping an arm around him.

"Talk to me," he said softly.

Landon hesitated before starting. "You know what's bothering me. We've been sleeping together for six months and that's all we do. We don't hang out like we used to. We don't play video games; we don't leave the house. You only come over at night and this is the first time I've been to your new place."

"So, you think this is just sex to me?" Kevin asked.

"It's what it seems like." Landon purposely looked away from him. "I've been wondering for months now if you still have a girlfriend or something. Even now I'm wondering if some chick is going to pop up over here tonight."

Kevin reached over to force Landon to face him. "There's no one else, male or female. I didn't bring you over here before because I moved in with nothing but my clothes and some blankets. I wanted to at least have something for us to lay on other than the floor before you came over. It wasn't because I'm hiding anything. But now I have to ask, do you have anyone else?"

Landon scowled. "Why the hell would you ask me that?"

"Because I know you. Any time you ever messed with someone and it's just sex to you, you keep three or four more in rotation. If you thought this was only sex, did you find someone else?"

Landon made sure to look him right in the eyes, so it would be clear he wasn't lying. "Hell no. I wouldn't do that to you."

"And I wouldn't do that to you. I've been around when the others messed around on you. We're together, and I'll never cheat on you." Kevin wiped a hand over his face in frustration. "I know I'm moving slow but I didn't stop caring when we started having sex."

"Yeah, but this is just an experiment to you."

Kevin stared at him for several seconds in disbelief before his face contorted with rage and he jumped off the futon. He started pacing and Landon could only stare at him. Finally, he stopped and looked back at him.

"Is that what you think this is, an experiment?" Kevin practically spat the last word.

"Well, isn't it?" Landon asked.

Kevin laughed a humorless laugh. "Ok, if you think it's an experiment, allow me to tell you the results." He leaned down to eye level with Landon, bracing himself on his arms on either side of him. "I don't know if I can really be called gay. I don't find other guys attractive. I don't get turned on by watching a gay porn. I don't look at other guys' asses or bulges. The only guy on the face of the earth that I'm attracted to is you. When I wake up, you're on my mind, even when I'm not lying next to you. I want you all the time. Sex with you is like none I've had before. Everything about you turns me on, even now when I'm pissed off. See?" He snatched Landon's hand and forced it onto his quite obvious erection. "No broad ever had this effect on me. No one gets me hard like this all the time. No one ever gave me any of the urges you do. I never checked up on broads like I check up on you. I didn't give a shit about any of them. You I give a shit about." He straightened up and walked off, leaving Landon alone in the living room.

"Holy shit," was all Landon could say. He'd never misread anyone before. He was a Magus, and humans had little to no mental defense. But he'd been wrong here, terribly so.

He waited a few seconds before following Kevin into the bedroom. Kevin was standing at the window, staring out of the open blinds at the building next to his. Landon wrapped his arms around his waist while laying his head on his back.

"I'm sorry."

Kevin sighed. "No, I'm sorry. The way you feel makes sense." He turned in Landon's arms so that they were facing each other. "It's my fault. I'm so new to all this and I don't know how to approach you now. When we were friends, you were so easy to talk to. Now, I don't know how to. It's just different now that we're together. You know what I'm saying?"

Landon chuckled. "No, not really. I'm still the same dude."

"I just feel like you deserve so much that I'm not ready to give. I can give you my body and my heart, even my soul. But I'm not ready to come out to everyone yet."

Landon looked up at him. "I'm not asking you to. I just want things to be normal again. I want to be like we were, just when we wager something on a game it can be sex instead of money." He grinned.

Kevin grinned back at him. "I can do that. So how about I kick your ass in some *Smackdown vs. Raw 2010*?"

Landon raised an eyebrow, all awkwardness from the previous conversation seemingly gone. "What's your wager?"

Kevin appeared to think for a few seconds. "How about we play an ironman match, and the loser is the winner's slave for the night?"

Landon laughed. "I'm so kicking your ass."

"I win either way." Kevin leaned down, forcefully taking his mouth in a kiss that Landon felt from head to toe. He hardened easily, his mind quickly going to things that could be done that night. Before it got too heavy, Kevin pulled back and let him go.

"Whoa," was all that Landon could say.

Kevin grinned again. "Now I know I'm gonna win."

He walked off, heading back into the living room with one hell of a bulge sticking out.

"The hell you are," Landon muttered.

Chapter Three

A one-hour ironman match was quite a challenge, even in a video game. Both had their own created wrestlers and had played down to one minute. Kevin was ahead 20 decisions to 19 and trying to get one last pinfall in.

"I got this won now," he bragged.

"Bullshit!" Landon shot back.

"Watch me." Kevin's character ran in, looking to hit his signature move.

Landon smirked as he countered and his character rolled Kevin's up in a pin.

"Shit!" Kevin frantically began pressing buttons to get his character to kick out. Unfortunately, it didn't happen and Landon tied the game up.

"It's a tie," Landon told him, still smirking.

"Bullshit, we've still got 30 seconds."

Landon shook his head and got into the last 30 seconds of the game. They ended with a tie, just as Landon predicted.

"So what now?" he asked.

"We go to sudden death," Kevin answered.

"No way."

Kevin put the controller down. "Ok, fine. How about this?" He leaned in and brought their lips together, this time in a softer kiss. He reached up and ran his fingers through Landon's hair as he kissed him. Reaching around with one arm, he lifted Landon up and sat him on his lap, never breaking the kiss. Landon broke away first, looking down at him.

"What are you doing?"

Kevin moved his hips slightly so that his erection poked at Landon. "Sorry, but I love having you on top of me."

"Really now?" Landon stood up between Kevin's legs, then leaned down and pushed him over to lie down. "I like my way better."

Kevin smiled. "This works too."

Landon lay down on top of him between his legs and smiled back at him. This peaked Kevin's curiosity.

"Why are you smiling?"

Landon shrugged. "Maybe I'm enjoying this."

Kevin lightly stroked his face. "We haven't started yet."

Landon's eyes flashed, hunger becoming apparent in his gaze. "Believe me, I know. Now lose the clothes."

Kevin laughed. "I see you're feeling bossy tonight."

"Damn straight. Now lose 'em."

"Yes sir." Kevin sat up enough to take off his shirt, then the chain. Landon sat back so that Kevin could remove his pants and underwear, leaving him totally naked. Landon's eyes immediately went to Kevin's dick, which was laying on his stomach. From there he had to admire that very nice six pack it was laying on. And finally his gaze went up to Kevin's face, which had a wide grin on it.

"It's yours, babe, do what you want."

Landon reached down and grabbed him, his fingertips just barely able to touch each other around the width of him. Although Landon was normally more of a top, Kevin made him enjoy being a bottom as well. He couldn't pinpoint what exactly made him enjoy Kevin so much. Maybe it was something about the width or the length of it. Or maybe it was just because it was Kevin. Either way, he enjoyed what he was about to do now.

Kevin sucked in his breath as Landon took him into his mouth. Landon was a pro at this, taking him in all the way to the base before coming back up to work on the head. Kevin's hand went to the back of his head, not to guide him but out of habit. Landon needed no guidance at all, as he was about to send Kevin into a frenzy. He reached to try to push Landon back, knowing he was getting close.

"Hold on babe," he gasped.

Landon chuckled around him and kept going.

"Wait, this isn't... Ah fuck!" Kevin gripped the back of Landon's head with both hands and arched his back as he came explosively. When he was finished, Landon pulled back with a laugh.

"It's always so amusing to make you cuss during sex," he commented.

Kevin fell back on the futon. "That wasn't how I meant that to happen."

"It's ok. We're far from done."

Kevin raised his head. "Say what?"

"There's this thing called marathon sex, which you've clearly never done before. You're about to learn all about it tonight." Landon grinned devilishly.

Kevin raised an eyebrow. "Marathon sex, huh? Sounds kinky."

Landon stood up. "Depends on how you do it. But I gotta go get something first." He turned to leave, then paused and looked back. "Stay there just like that."

Kevin laughed. "OK."

Landon went out to his car and opened the trunk. Reaching inside, he searched for the box of condoms he'd thrown there a few days before. He liked to stay prepared after all. He found it in the very back of the trunk and pulled it out, along with a bottle of lube. His hand brushed up against a lockbox that he also kept in his trunk. He stared at it for a few seconds, his thoughts going to what he kept in it. Snapping out of his trance, he took what he'd come for and closed the trunk.

Back in the apartment, Kevin had let the futon down to a bed and was lying across it. Landon closed the door and sat down next to him.

"So what's next?" Kevin asked.

"That depends entirely on you. What do you want to do?"

Kevin spent a few seconds thinking. "Take off your clothes."

Landon rose to do so.

"Slowly," Kevin added.

Landon laughed. "If you wanted a show, we should have put on music."

"You asked what I wanted," Kevin reminded him.

Well, he couldn't argue that. Landon began to undress slowly, starting by kicking off his shoes. Then he unfastened his belt and slowly lowered his pants to step out of them. Next went the underwear and he slowly raised his shirt before pulling it off. Kevin grinned as he watched, then looked him over. Landon clearly worked out, as he had his own six pack. His nipples were hard and so was another part of him.

"Come stand over here," Kevin ordered, pointing in front of him.

Landon did as he was told and Kevin sat up in front of him. Kevin gripped him by the hips, enjoying the dimple between his leg and groin area. He leaned forward and took Landon into his mouth while reaching around to grab his ass, which was much bigger than it appeared to be when he was dressed. Kevin let his hands roam as his mouth worked and Landon threw his head back and closed his eyes, enjoying the sensations. Kevin grabbed two handfuls of ass and pulled him forward, then relaxed his hands. Landon knew the signal and pulled back, then pushed forward slowly. He opened his eyes and looked down, noticing Kevin had gotten hard again. He continued moving back and forth, or in and out as the case may be, careful not to go too far. The feeling was great, and he would have been content to continue this way. He closed his eyes again and as he did, one of Kevin's hands released him and reached down to the floor. Landon opened his eyes once more and watched him take out one of the condoms and grab the lube before pulling back off him. Landon raised an eyebrow, surprised when Kevin put the condom on him instead of himself, then applied some of the lube. Kevin stood and pushed Landon onto the futon, then straddled him.

"Are you sure about this?" Landon asked.

"Yeah." Kevin leaned down and kissed him while positioning Landon to enter him. Breaking the kiss, he sat back enough for the head to slide in. He hissed at the slight pain of entry and paused.

"You don't have to do this," Landon told him.

Kevin, who had closed his eyes, opened them to look down at him. "I want to."

They had tried before and it had been too painful for Kevin, so Landon remained skeptical. "OK, ease back."

He reached up and took hold of Kevin's waist, holding him to prevent him from taking too much too quickly. He didn't have the width Kevin had, but to someone not as experienced, it was still a lot to take, and even some experienced people had difficulty. Honestly this was torture for Landon, but there were far worse ways to be tortured. He held himself back as Kevin slowly took him in. Landon sat up and Kevin wrapped his legs around his waist while taking a moment to adjust to the intrusion. Landon reached up to cup the back of his head and kissed him.

Kevin finally felt more comfortable and began to move, slowly at first since he was unsure of himself. Landon moved his hands to grip Kevin's lower back and ass, which also gave him a better angle. Kevin moaned and began to move faster, finding himself enjoying this new sensation. Whatever spot Landon was hitting felt great and to his surprise, he felt close to release again. Wanting to hold off, he tried to slow down only for Landon to grab on tighter and urge him on, faster and faster. Kevin braced himself by putting both hands on Landon's knees and then arching his back. This worked even better for Landon, who began to pump into him. Kevin leaned his head back and rode, eyes closed and his erection standing straight up.

Landon moaned and pulled Kevin closer, their lips meeting again. As they did, Kevin came again with a loud moan and reflexively tightened around Landon with each spurt. Landon grabbed his hips with both hands and slammed in one last time as he came.

Kevin leaned his head forward to rest on Landon's shoulder as the aftershocks wore off. Landon ran his hands up and down Kevin's back and held him, kissing his neck affectionately.

"That was interesting," Kevin commented.

Landon laughed softly against his neck. "That was great."

Kevin straightened up and looked down at him. "Looks like I made a mess."

Landon laughed again. "No one ever said sex was clean. That's what showers are for."

Kevin slowly rose up on his knees, forcing Landon out before standing. His legs were a little weak and he took a few seconds to steady himself. Landon stood up with him, placing his hand on his lower back and rubbing in a soothing gesture.

"Let's go take one then," Kevin told him.

Chapter Four

Landon stepped under the warm spray of the shower first. Kevin followed a few seconds later, handing him a washcloth. Landon grabbed the bar of soap from its holder and lathered the rag, then began to wash Kevin instead of himself.

"What are you doing?" Kevin asked.

"What does it look like?" Landon replied.

Kevin decided it was easier, and frankly more interesting, to just let it happen. Landon took his time, starting at Kevin's neck and working his way down his chest and stomach, down to his groin where he took a little more time. He turned Kevin around to clean the other side, being extra careful as he knew Kevin would be sore. Kevin winced once, prompting Landon to look closer. Fortunately, he saw nothing to worry about and worked his way up, washing his back before letting him step under the spray. Kevin turned back around to face him.

"It's your turn."

Landon smirked. "OK."

Kevin began to return the favor, working in an identical way. He did linger longer around Landon's ass, which made Landon laugh. That was Kevin's favorite part of his body, so he should have known he'd stay there longer.

Finally Kevin let him step under the water to rinse off. Under the spray, Landon turned to face him again and Kevin quickly leaned down to kiss him. He wrapped his arm around Landon's waist and brought their bodies together. To Landon's continued amusement, Kevin was getting hard again, so he pulled away.

"I see you're getting the idea of marathon sex." He reached down and gripped him. "You're ready for another round."

Kevin grinned. "You started it. So let's go work on the next round."

Landon laughed as he turned the water off. Kevin stepped out first and handed him a towel. As he dried off, Landon noticed Kevin just staring at him.

"Are you going to dry off or just stand there staring?" Landon asked.

"Sorry, I was just thinking." Kevin began to dry himself off. "About what?"

"About how different this is." Kevin hung his towel up. "It's not a bad thing. It just takes some getting used to."

Landon didn't respond, choosing to walk out of the bathroom and back to the futon. Kevin followed and sat next to him.

"Don't be like that." He brushed a dreadlock back from Landon's face. "You know how I was before. It's so different with you. I mean, everything is different. I feel different with you."

"What do you mean?" Landon asked.

"I mean it's different. It strikes me sometimes just how much more I like you than anyone else. I actually like doing things like watching you dry off, and that's really not like me. And my sex drive is higher than ever."

"Really now? Care to demonstrate?" Landon wiggled his eyebrows.

He was pretty sure Kevin actually growled at him. Before he knew it, Kevin had flipped him over and put him onto his knees. Landon laughed, then moaned as Kevin knelt behind him and his tongue entered him. There was no laughing now as Kevin went to work, first working in a circle, and then going in and out repeatedly. Landon clenched the mattress in his fists and bit his lip, holding back any sound he might make. That only made Kevin work harder. He knew Landon tried to always stay quiet out of an old habit from his teenage days, but he also knew he could make Landon do what he wanted. He wanted at least another moan before he stopped, and he knew how to get it.

Kevin flipped himself onto his back and put his head between Landon's legs. He then took Landon's full erection into his mouth while placing one finger at his entrance. Beginning to suck, he inserted his finger slowly and got the moan he wanted, but he wanted more. He kept going, working both his finger and his mouth together. Landon's breathing got heavy as he was getting close and trying to hold back.

"Shit!" Landon exclaimed as he exploded.

Kevin kept going until Landon was completely finished, then lifted Landon up and sat him on his lap as he sat up.

"Wow," Landon commented breathlessly.

Kevin kissed him briefly. "I had to even the score."

Landon noticed Kevin's hands moving behind him. "What are you doing?"

"Giving you what you want," Kevin answered.

Landon looked back, discovering Kevin had put on a condom and lube. "I'm going to be sore as hell tomorrow."

Kevin grinned. "You wanted it."

DRAKO

Landon didn't respond verbally. He rose up on his knees to position himself to allow Kevin's entrance. He bit his lip as Kevin pushed the head in, then he slowly lowered himself until Kevin was completely inside. Landon remained still, giving his body time to adjust and Kevin began to kiss him softly. He was careful not to move, letting Landon move at his own pace. It didn't take long for Landon to begin to move, pushing himself up until only the head was in, then lowering himself again. He did this several times, enjoying the sensation of Kevin sliding in and out, as well as the look on Kevin's face.

That look was one of sheer male delight. He loved watching Landon like this and sometimes felt as if he could watch this all day. However, as Landon came down one last time, Kevin wrapped his arms around him, bracing himself for the ride he knew was coming. Landon began to grind, slowly at first and gradually picking up speed. His eyes were closed, as if he was concentrating. Kevin watched him the whole time, waiting for him to open his eyes. Landon did, looking right into Kevin's big brown eyes. Kevin needed that, needed to see all of this man he was with. This is how he accepted it, and how he knew what he was doing wasn't a mistake. This was no passing fling. It wasn't an interest that would die with time, and it wasn't him feeling sorry for his friend. All that he felt was love for this man. With a moan he leaned forward and captured Landon's lips again.

Landon felt Kevin running his hands up and down his back, knowing Kevin loved the way his back arched. As Landon broke their kiss and leaned his head back, Kevin's lips went to his neck, kissing lightly at first and then biting. Landon moaned, the mix of pleasure and pain driving him close to the edge. He moved just enough to capture Kevin's lips again as he began to move faster. He cried out as he came, clenching down on Kevin. Kevin came as well with an even louder cry, then laid his head on Landon's chest as he held him. And to think, their night was just getting started.

During the night, Landon felt his dreams shift. He knew he was no longer in a dream. His spirit was being called home. He could not resist. An order from a Magus King was absolute, especially in the weakened state of sleep. In seconds, he stood before a large silver throne. On it sat a beautiful man, appearing closer to middle aged, with long black and silver hair. His head rested on the right hand and piercing emerald green eyes stared at him passively. The broad shouldered male was quite a bit larger than Landon and muscular. His beauty was almost painful to behold in the eyes of mortals. He was dressed in a simple, long silver robe, and knowing him he most likely wore nothing else underneath it. His full, red lips curved into a smile at the sight of Landon. The king of Avalon, Damien Adaire, was in a strangely amused mood.

"My lord?" Landon questioned, silently hating deferring to the older male.

"Your escapades with that mortal are most entertaining to watch. You have such prowess. It's a shame I could not get you to lie with me in such a way."

Landon scowled. "Firstly, it's perverse that you'd be watching. Secondly, I'm sure that's not why you called me here when I could be waking up and doing it again."

The king laughed. "Of course it isn't, but I can always hope you'll cave in. Besides, you are my warrior. I am always watching."

"No offense, but don't you have a queen to take up time with instead of watching me?"

Damien shrugged. "Yes, I do. And I will most likely take her once I am done with you. You have a task to do and you're not moving about it fast enough."

"It was my understanding that I was to live my own life as well as guard your son. He's only half Magus. I can't rush him into his heritage."

"I'm aware of the terms of your time in the mortal world, but remember this. You owe me for covering up your dirty little secret." Damien waved a hand and the normally dulled beauty Landon himself possessed came to the full surface. His eyes changed from their usual brown to a bright and vibrant green. Cool energy flowed through his body, sharpening his muscle definition. His cheekbones were slightly higher and more pronounced and his skin held a slight sheen to it, almost a glow.

"Did you just release the rest of my power?" Landon asked.

"I released some of it, yes. It's been so long since you've had it that you've forgotten how powerful you truly are. The fiercest of my warriors. Though this body you inhabit is young, you yourself are so much older. Your reincarnation into this form has been pleasing, but even reincarnated, you have innate beauty. Not the same as my own. You have more of a rugged look. Even released from the bonds you appear more human. That is why I chose you to bring my son to me."

"I'm well aware of what you want me to do. But why the release?"

"Because the past will always catch up with you. I can't have you dying on me. Try not to be a self-sacrificing fool this time."

SHADOWS OF THE PAST

The King rose from his throne. "There are other forces at work in the area. I need you to be able to face them. But keep the human at your side. He intrigues me."

"You're meddling. Do you know something more than what I know about this relationship?" Landon asked.

Damien chuckled. "So suspicious. I see no grand destiny, if that's the type of answer you're looking for. But he will be a source of strength for you."

"He's a mortal. No mortal, no matter how close I may be to him, will be a source of strength to me."

Damien shook his head. "Do not try to act so cold and uncaring with me. I know better. My enemies are on the move and at some point you will need to return here. First, you must protect my son and his mother at all costs. Your past and mine endanger them. You'd do well to remember that."

Before he could respond, Landon suddenly had the sensation of falling, right before his spirit slammed back into his body, shaking the bed in which he lay. Fortunately, Kevin remained asleep, merely pulling him closer. Landon sighed and waited for sleep to claim him again.

Chapter Five

Landon was awakened the next morning by his phone ringing. He untangled himself from Kevin and looked at the caller ID. The name of the teen he'd been discussing with Damien was showing, so he answered.

"Shouldn't you be in school, Brian?" he asked.

"Dude, I'm off today for a staff development day," Brian replied.

"Well, what's up, kid?"

"I want to get out of the house. Are you busy?"

Landon glanced at his phone to check the time. "Give me a few minutes."

"Thanks, bro." Brian hung up.

Sighing softly, Landon got up and began to get dressed.

"Were you going to tell me you're leaving?"

Landon turned back to Kevin, who was propped up on his elbow looking at him. "Of course, I was. You have to get up and lock the door behind me."

Hurt flashed in Kevin's eyes, but he masked his emotions quickly. "Is that the only reason?"

Landon realized the error in his wording. He'd have to be more careful and start taking Kevin more seriously. As such, he leaned back across the bed and kissed him soundly.

"There's that too."

Kevin smiled. "Where are you off to?"

"Brian is out of school and wants to hang out. I assume that means he needs to talk."

"Okay, text me later."

Landon smiled and left out. Kevin fell back on the bed with a groan. He'd wanted to spend the day with Landon alone, but he knew Landon had a big sense of responsibility towards all his loved ones. This time, Kevin would have to wait. He shouldn't complain, really. He'd had Landon to himself all night, and technically he'd be feeling the effects of that night all day and for several more to come. He couldn't help but smile. He'd eventually get a whole day to himself with Landon, and he'd make it count. After all, he couldn't let Landon continue thinking that this thing between them was only sexual. Landon deserved more, and Kevin would be damned if he let him get tired of him and look for more with someone else.

Landon pulled up in front of Brian's house and blew the horn. A few seconds later, the sixteen-year-old ran out and hopped in the car. He was a little shorter than Landon and skinnier, with large dark brown eyes and caramel brown skin. He kept his hair cut low normally, although at the moment it had grown out and he could use another cut. He wore slim square framed glasses and had just thrown on a simple blue t-shirt and blue jeans.

"What did you want to do today, kid?" Landon asked. "Maybe get a haircut?"

"I don't get paid until next week, so I'll wait," Brian answered.

Landon rolled his eyes. "You know I don't let you pay for anything when we're together. Do you want a haircut or not?"

Brian shrugged. "I guess."

DRAKO

Landon began to drive. "So, how's school going?"

"It's going okay, I guess."

"What's with all the guessing?" Landon questioned.

"Well, I'm not the most popular guy around, but my grades are good."

Landon frowned. "Any particular problems?"

"No, I'm just single. Not many out guys at my school."

Landon relaxed. "Boyfriends come in time. Don't stress yourself over it."

Brian snorted. "At the rate I'm going I'll be in college before I finally get an actual boyfriend."

Landon laughed. "I could live with that."

"I can't," Brian mumbled.

Landon reached over and took Brian's hand in his own. "Hey, high school is tough enough as a gay black teenager. Adding a boyfriend to the mix makes it harder, especially if they're a closet case."

Brian merely looked out the window without answering. Landon glanced over.

"Seriously, give it time. Don't try to push yourself into your first gay relationship."

"Well, I kind of have a crush on a guy but he's so hard to approach." Brian actually blushed. "I know he's gay. I just don't know how to approach him."

"So you're just too shy to ask him out?" Landon smiled. "I was like that in high school. You just have to get it over with. It gets easier after the first time."

"I hope so."

"What's his name and what does he look like?" Landon asked.

Brian finally turned back to look at him. "Why?"

"So I know whose ass to kick if he breaks your heart," Landon answered.

Brian laughed. "His name is Leon and he's about my height. Closer to your size but a little darker. Kind of nerdy, like me. Nice lips too."

Landon laughed again. "You've been around me too much, kid, if a guy's lips are a main attraction."

"I can't help it. They're big and soft, but not disgustingly big. He doesn't look like he'll try to swallow my face."

Landon shook his head. "If I were older I'd wonder if you were actually my kid. So, does your mom know yet?"

"No, I don't want to tell her. She's still getting past the fact that I had girlfriends before and that I'm not a virgin. No need to tell her I'm actually gay."

Landon shrugged, knowing there was no point trying to persuade him. The teen would tell his mother in his own time. But then his mother had something to tell him too.

Finally, he pulled up to a barber shop and released Brian's hand so that they could get out. Landon took notice of a black Cadillac Deville with tinted windows as they walked past. Thinking that it was just a nice car, he ignored it and led the way inside. Walking inside, they stopped at the front desk. Standing at the desk was a tall light skinned guy in a long sleeved baggy white shirt and black baggy jeans, which even from where he was Landon could tell were sagging. The man's hazel eyes lingered on Brian a little too long, so Landon leaned in close.

"Don't you recognize jailbait when you see it?" he spoke low so only the man heard him.

"My bad," the man answered. "What y'all need today?"

"The kid needs a haircut and a lining," Landon told him.

"A'ight. Come on back." The guy walked off.

Landon leaned towards Brian. "Do not flirt back with that dude. I'd hate to have to hurt him."

Brian shook his head and followed the man back to his chair, having no real idea just how serious Landon was. Landon took a seat in the waiting area just as a text from Kevin came through.

What time r we going 2 Renee's?

Landon sent a text to Renee first before answering. When she responded, he answered Kevin.

Any time after 4.

Landon looked down the aisle, watching the barber as he cut Brian's hair. Brian's eyes were closed and he wasn't talking, so at least Landon didn't have to worry about the older man flirting. That made it easy to turn his attention to Kevin's text.

Might be a little late. Got called in to work.

Ok, Landon typed back and closed his phone.

It didn't take long for the barber to finish. Landon paid the man and took his change back, then led Brian to the car. Upon examining his change, he found a slip of paper with writing on it. The writing was a name, Xavier, and phone number along with a message to text him.

"Wow, I guess he liked you," Brian commented.

Landon stuffed the paper in his wallet along with the change. "Too bad he's not my type and I'm not single. Otherwise, he'd be good for a quick screw and that's all."

Brian laughed. "You're so rude."

Landon shrugged. "DL guys are hard to be with. Most have one purpose, as a hole to plow or someone to plow you, depending on the preference."

"If I were older, I'd go for it."

Landon snorted. "Take my advice kid, and be very selective with your partners. DL guys can bring more drama than they're worth if they never plan to come out of the closet."

"Speaking of which, aren't you with a closet case?" Brian asked.

Landon sighed. "Yeah, something like that. He's a little different, since he was straight before me. Never had a gay urge until me. He brings a whole different set of problems."

"Like what?"

"Mostly getting him to treat me the way I want and not like some sideline. Kevin wasn't a relationship-oriented guy before me so despite his best intentions, I've been relegated to being at home."

"I'm surprised you're still with him."

Landon smirked. "He's trying. Like most straight guys, he didn't realize what he was doing was wrong. So we'll just see how it goes."

"You two were friends before, right?"

Landon nodded. "Yeah, he'd seen me go through a lot with my exes. Somehow he developed feelings for me, feelings that I can't question after last night."

"So then, it's going well for you?" Brian questioned.

"I think it'll get better," Landon answered. "Now understand that I'm not telling you to never date a DL guy. That's your choice. I just want you to keep in mind the problems they can bring."

"It's okay. I think I'd rather have someone more like you. Just not you," Brian added quickly.

"You saying there's something wrong with me?" Landon joked.

Brian rolled his eyes, playing along. "Yeah, you're old."

"I'm only twenty-three."

"Yeah, and I'm sixteen."

"Oh yeah."

They both laughed.

"So, Kevin and I are going to dinner at Renee's tonight. Do you want to come?" Landon asked.

"I'm always up for free food," Brian answered.

"Well, that's hours away. So, let's go get something to eat now to tie us over."

Chapter Six

"So, what are you cooking?" Landon asked.

He sat in Renee's living room looking at her moving around in the kitchen. Brian was curled up next to him and he had an arm around him.

"Baked lasagna," Renee told him. "And some garlic bread."

A couple of minutes later she came to join them in the living room.

"It should be ready in a little while." Renee looked to Brian. "So, how's life these days?"

Brian gave a shrug. "It's life."

"Which translates to it sucks to him," Landon added.

Renee laughed. "Life in general sucks, but we have good times."

"Of course, we do. We accept the inevitability of bullshit and therefore are mostly prepared for it when it comes our way." Landon squeezed Brian's shoulder. "But his life isn't so bad. He's just shy and giving himself hell over it."

Brian scowled at him as Renee perked up.

"This must mean there's a boy. Spill it kid," she ordered.

"I so hate you," Brian told Landon.

Landon laughed. "This is what you get for calling me your big brother. I torment relentlessly."

Brian rolled his eyes and looked to Renee. "It's not that big a deal. I just have to get the nerve to ask this guy out."

"Oh no, you don't get off easy with me. I want to know who he is and what he looks like, and if it gets serious, I need his whole legal name, address, and social security number."

Brian looked confused. "Why all that?"

"I like to have details on people that prevent them from hiding when I have to hunt them down and murder them for messing with what's mine," Renee answered.

Landon laughed again. "I forgot about asking for the address and social. I must be slippin' in my old age."

"Damn straight you are. Good thing I'm not. So, out with the details, kid."

Landon listened with genuine amusement as Brian told her about the Leon guy he was now interested in. Of course, he didn't have the last two things she'd asked for, but Renee simply told him she'd get it herself when she met him.

"What do you mean, when you meet him?" Brian asked.

"What? You thought we'd just let you date this guy and never meet him?" Renee shook her head. "Oh no. We're obligated to grill the shit out of him until we're content that he's too scared to hurt you."

"And if he does it anyway, at least he'll be prepared for what happens to him afterward, since we gave him the warning," Landon added on.

Brian shook his head. "You're both nuts."

Landon nodded vigorously. "Totally fucking certifiable, kid. And unlike other people, we don't suffer from insanity. We enjoy it."

"Oh spectacularly," Renee added in an almost dreamy voice.

The laughter couldn't be held back from any of the three. When they finally recovered, Renee turned to Landon.

"Now that we've thoroughly scared the child of the group, it's time to talk about you. How'd everything go with Kevin?" she asked.

Landon shrugged. "He's trying, I guess. I can't really comment until I see how he does the next few weeks."

"Meanwhile, he got a number from the guy that cut my hair today," Brian told her.

Renee raised an eyebrow. "Oh, do tell."

Landon scowled at Brian. "You suck for that."

Brian shrugged. "Payback's a bitch."

Landon couldn't argue that logic.

"I'm waiting," Renee told him, an amused glint in her eyes.

"There's nothing to tell. It's just some DL guy. Not like he'd be worth my time."

Renee clearly didn't believe him. "You kept the number, didn't you?"

Landon didn't answer.

"Which means I'm right and you're keeping it as a backup in case Kevin screws up."

Landon shrugged. "Never hurts to have backup. But he'd only ever be something to screw once, maybe twice if he's good, and then leave. Not getting caught up with another closest case if this one doesn't work out."

Renee rolled her eyes. "Dude, half the guys you screw around with when you're single are DL and you know it."

"Yeah, and I make a point to fuck 'em and leave 'em," Landon replied.

Brian shook his head again. "Good thing I'm not some sweet little virgin or you'd be hurting my ears with this non-virgin language and philosophy."

Landon and Renee couldn't help but laugh at the joke. There was no sheltering those old enough to make adult decisions in their group. And besides, they knew Brian was just as bad as they were, at least as far as his language went.

"So seriously, you really wouldn't go for another one of these DL guys?" Renee asked.

"You know I never liked them before."

"So you'd rather have a flamer?" she teased.

Landon scowled. "What might I do with a flamer? I don't need a man that's forgotten he's a man. Nothing worse than a guy that takes longer than any two chicks to get ready to go out, and has an attitude worse than any chick on her period. At least women have a reason to be a bitch one week out of the month. They bleed for seven days. Men have no such excuse."

Renee and Brian laughed. As the laughter died out, they heard a knock at the door.

"That must be Kevin." Renee went to answer the door.

A few seconds later, the two came in. Kevin's eyes went straight to Landon and he walked right over, then leaned down and captured his lips quickly. Landon's eyes widened in surprise as he accepted the kiss and he barely felt Brian leave from under his arm. After what felt like minutes but was really only a few seconds, Kevin pulled back with a grin.

"Hi," he said cheerfully.

"Uh, hi," Landon managed to respond.

Kevin sat down on his free side and wrapped an arm around him as if this was normal for them. He'd never kissed Landon in front of anyone else, even though Renee and Brian knew how long they'd been together. Brian sat off a little further to the side as Renee took her original seat with eyebrows raised. Kevin ignored the signs of obvious curiosity as if he didn't see them.

"So, we're not going to talk about that, are we?" Renee asked.

Kevin looked at her. "Talk about what?"

"Ooookay, and moving on," Renee responded.

Brian chuckled and Landon was just confused.

"Hey, Brian, come help me in the kitchen," Renee ordered as she stood and left the room.

Brian got up and followed, leaving the couple alone together.

"What was that?" Landon asked Kevin once they were out of the room.

Kevin gave him a bland stare. "Didn't think you'd need me to explain when I kiss you."

"I do when you've never done it in front of people before," Landon replied.

"I'm just trying to open up and be what you need, and this is a small step that I can take comfortably." Kevin looked him in the eyes. "I've got a lot to work on to start making you happy. I can't just keep you to myself at night and expect you to be satisfied with that."

"So that was your way of making me happy?" Landon questioned.

"It's a start. It worked, didn't it?"

"Well, yeah, it did," Landon admitted.

"Then I've gotten off to a good start." Kevin smiled. "I know I'm not real experienced with this relationship thing, but I kind of realized I was going to lose you soon. And I really hate that idea."

Landon couldn't help but smile back. "Well, thank you. But you don't have to push yourself faster than you're ready to go."

"You know, that's why I love you so much. You've clearly been suffering in this relationship because I'm not giving you everything you need but you're still more worried about me. I don't know how you do it."

Landon hoped he wasn't blushing, but he obviously was. "It's just the way I am when I love someone, Kevin. I don't really think that much about myself. And you're a special circumstance since this whole lifestyle is new for you."

Kevin shook his head. "Don't make excuses for me. If I'm screwing up, I want to know. Treat me the same as you treated any of your exes. Just without the dumping me part."

Landon smirked. "As long as you're faithful, that's not an issue."

"Me being with anyone else as long as you want me is not an issue."

Well, if that didn't just make a guy feel special what would? Landon couldn't resist the urge to kiss him again, so he did it. If they'd been alone, this would have ended with nice, hot steamy sex. Then again, after the night before, he should probably refrain from sex for another day or two.

"Food's ready guys!" Renee called.

Landon broke the kiss and as he looked into Kevin's eyes, he knew full well he wasn't getting a break from sex tonight either. Funny how the thought made him want to rush through dinner to get home. He wouldn't though, because he valued time spent with his friends too. Besides, making Kevin wait couldn't hurt, could it?

Kevin stood up and readjusted his erection, which he'd been unable to prevent as soon as Landon's lips met his. Landon bit his lip and once again fought the urge to speed through dinner. It was hard to tell who this was going to bother the most.

In the kitchen, Kevin sat on Landon's right and Brian on his left, while Renee sat opposite of him. Finally, it was time to eat and they all dug in.

"I take it from the fact that no one is talking that it's good, right?" Renee answered.

"You know I wouldn't eat it if it wasn't good," Landon answered.

"It's great," Brian said around his food.

"What he said," Kevin added.

Renee laughed. "Thanks guys."

"Thank you," Brian responded as he continued to scarf down the food.

Landon continued eating but he watched Brian. It had been a while since his young friend had seemed truly happy. Perhaps he needed to spend even more time with him, because he was definitely happy tonight. Something else was bothering that boy that he wouldn't tell anyone yet.

Kevin watched Landon as he ate. Something was on his lover's mind, and he knew it had something to do with Brian, his little brother by Landon's standards. Kevin knew they were just friends and knew that Brian often called Landon bro. He knew Landon liked the idea of being Brian's big brother figure. What he didn't know was what was going on that would bother Landon so much and he intended to find out as soon as they were alone.

Finally, Brian finished his meal off and sat back in contentment. "I think I'm full."

Renee smiled at him. "Take some home too. There's more than enough."

Brian beamed. "Thanks!"

Landon and Kevin finished up their meal as well. Landon checked the time.

"Looks like we got a decent amount of time before the kid has to go home. So what will we do for fun?"

Renee stood and went to a drawer, pulling out a deck of Uno cards. "Blast from the past right?"

Landon grinned. "I'm so game for that."

"I'm in," Kevin spoke up.

"Me too," Brian added.

"Oh, I'm so thrashing the shit out of you guys in this. Clear the table and let the beating commence."

Chapter Seven

Later that evening, Landon drove Brian home. He stopped in front of his house and waited.

"Did you have fun tonight?" he asked.

Brian nodded. "It was good to get out of the house."

"So, are you going to tell me what's really been bothering you?"

Brian stiffened. "Nothing else is bothering me."

"Don't lie to me," Landon told him in a low voice.

"I'm fine, really."

Landon wrapped an arm around his shoulder and pulled him in to a hug. "I know you're not telling me what's really wrong, but it's okay." Landon pulled away. "Go on in, kid. And call me when you get out of school tomorrow."

Brian smiled and got out of the car. Landon pulled out his phone as a text came through. Not surprisingly, it was Kevin.

Come to my house.

Landon smirked and pulled off, heading to do as told.

Landon stood outside Kevin's door, waiting for him to answer. Finally, Kevin answered, with a smile. He stepped aside to let Landon in and closed the door behind him. Landon took a seat on the futon and looked up at Kevin expectantly.

"This wasn't a sex call," Kevin told him.

Landon raised an eyebrow in question. "Really?"

Kevin sat next to him. "No, I just want time with you. I had hoped to spend today with you but you had to take Brian out. I was hoping to at least get a couple of hours in with you now."

"Only a couple of hours?"

"Well, yeah. I made plans earlier to go out with some of the boys. So, I figured I could get a little time in with you before I go."

Landon looked skeptical. "Ok, and what are we supposed to do with this time together?"

Kevin shrugged. "I want things to be easy between us again. So, let's play a video game and just talk like we used to."

Landon gave a slight smirk. "It can't be exactly the same you know. I don't have anyone else to bitch about."

Kevin smiled again. "You've got me to bitch about. You can tell me all about the things I do wrong and how you'd like them fixed."

Landon laughed. "Start the game up then."

Kevin had switched from the wrestling game they'd played the night before to *Tekken 6*. As a more standard fighting game, it required less concentration, so they were free to talk.

"So, are you going to start talking yet?" Kevin asked.

"What's there to talk about?" Landon replied. "You're not doing anything wrong."

Kevin snorted. "Don't lie. I know when things are bothering you."

"I'm not lying. We had this talk last night. There's no point in repeating the same things when you haven't had time to work on it."

Kevin had to concede that point. "Ok, but something was bothering you at dinner tonight."

Landon sighed. "Yeah, Brian is hiding something from me. I can't shake the feeling that it's something big, something he doesn't need to keep to himself."

"What makes you say that?"

Landon took a few seconds to think about his reply before he spoke. "It's just a feeling really. In the past couple of years, I've gotten to know him pretty well. I can always tell when he's holding back. I have that feeling, but I can't tell what it is."

"He'll tell you eventually, won't he?" Kevin asked.

"Normally I'd say yes, but I'm afraid it'll be too late. I don't want anything bad to happen to him. He's been through some pretty rough things already."

As the current round ended, Kevin looked over at him. "What kind of things?"

"Some abuse when he was younger. That's kind of how we bonded. Birds of a feather and all."

Kevin paused the game. "What?"

Landon sighed. "I don't like to talk about it, but it's why I have some weird quirks."

Kevin put the controller down. "You're going to have to explain that one."

Landon cursed low, not really wanting to go into this topic. "Look, I don't want to go into detail but I have a history of sexual abuse when I was a young. Brian has the same type of history."

"Why are you just now telling me this?" Kevin asked.

"I don't talk about it. We all have skeletons in our closet and that's one I prefer not to dwell on."

"So are you saying it doesn't still bother you?"

Landon shook his head. "No, that would be a lie. It's a dark and painful part of my past that will always be there in the back of my mind. I merely choose not to dwell on it while I'm awake. I get enough reminders of it on occasion in my sleep."

Kevin realized this was a sensitive subject, and now that he knew he wanted to know more. He also knew better than to push too hard, as Landon would shut him out if he did.

"Anyway, the point is that Brian shuts himself off a lot when things are going wrong. He's so used to not having anyone to talk to that he just holds it all in. Even after all this time, he has a hard time telling me the things that really bother him."

"He sounds like someone else I know," Kevin commented.

Landon glared at him. "I tell you plenty of things."

"Yet you never told me about the abuse in your past. Don't you think we've known each other long enough for you to tell me about it?"

Landon sighed. "I told you, I just don't talk about it."

Kevin gave him a skeptical look. "Yeah, I'm sure. It's alright, though."

"It was a long time ago and I went through plenty of counselling to get past it, but it'll always be with me in life. No matter how good things are going, every now and then I get nightmares about it. I relive it in dreams. That's why I was an insomniac in high school and every now and then I go for long periods where I don't sleep much. I even wake up in the middle of the night sometimes and it takes a while to remember that I'm an adult now and it's not happening all over again."

"Can I ask who did it?"

Landon took a few seconds to respond. "It was my father's wife. In her twisted mind, she was getting back at my mother and father for having me. She says I was the child that wasn't supposed to exist. And of course that stuck with me for years."

That left Kevin at a loss for words. He couldn't fathom the logic behind hurting a child to get back at the parents. And he had no idea what to say to Landon now, as he had the urge to say something comforting but had no clue what could possibly comfort someone dealing with that. Landon smiled at him.

"I know, it's hard to understand. I don't really get it either. I only know what she told me when she did it. She didn't really care about me at all. I was merely her tool to get back at my parents."

"What happened to her?" Kevin asked.

Landon shrugged. "I know my father stayed with her after I finally told him about it. Told me I was a liar. She admitted it later down the road, so he generally feels like an ass. But she's still alive somewhere and as long as she's far away from me then I really don't care." That was close enough to the truth anyway. The fact is he was a Magus and so were his father and the woman responsible for that particular dark part of his past in this lifetime. Magi could be just as jaded, if not more so, than humans.

"So what about Brian?"

"I won't share details of his story. That's his story to tell, but it's pretty similar to mine. Same issue and time frame. Different people."

Kevin understood that he wasn't going to get anything else out of Landon, so he switched topics. "Well, since I've got a couple hours left, why don't we just sit here and watch a movie together?"

"Works for me," Landon replied.

Kevin turned off the game and went to look over his selection of movies. "Do you have a preference of movies?"

"As long as it's not comedy, I'm fine with it."

Kevin smirked and went through his movies, looking for anything of Landon's favorite genre. Finally, he pulled out a movie and held it up for Landon to see.

"Halloween?" Landon laughed. "I'm always up for horror movies. It's so fun to see people run and trip over nothing so the serial killer catches them and hacks them to pieces."

Kevin laughed and put the movie in before joining him on the futon again. "You have a twisted sense of humor." He put an arm around Landon and pulled him close.

"Yeah well you like it," Landon joked.

Kevin kissed his forehead. "Yeah, I do."

Chapter Eight

Landon had gone home while Kevin went out. He slept the night away and awoke late the next morning. Knowing he had to work, he called Kevin and got no answer. He had a feeling that he was missing something. Over the years, he'd had this nagging feeling before, that feeling deep down that the person he was with was up to no good. It had nothing to do with the fact that he was a Magus warrior either. This intuition didn't come from any mystical powers. It was just a gut feeling that turned out to be right more often than not. He'd learned to trust that feeling. In his mind, he knew that to go looking for trouble is to find it. But he couldn't resist the urge, and so he went to Kevin's house. Kevin's car was there, which meant he was home. He sat in the car for several minutes, debating on his course of action. Kevin could be asleep after all. But something told him that wasn't the case.

Finally resolving himself, Landon stepped out of the car and went to the door. He knocked and waited, listening. He could hear movement inside, and there was definitely more than one person inside. He heard voices, two distinct male voices that he recognized. One was Kevin, and the other was Kevin's friend Johnny. That didn't bother him. What did bother him were the female voices he heard along with them.

After what seemed like forever, Kevin opened the door. He wasn't wearing a shirt and only a pair of basketball shorts, and he'd clearly just woken up. His eyes widened when he saw

Landon standing there, and Landon took a cursory glance over his shoulder.

"Guess there's no need to ask how you're feeling. Looks like you had plenty of fun last night."

"It's not what it looks like," Kevin told him.

Landon laughed humorlessly. "Do I look stupid to you? There's no way this isn't what it looks like. But whatever, I'm gone."

He turned and walked off.

"Shit!" Kevin swore under his breath.

Johnny came up behind him. "Yo, who was that?"

"It was Landon." Kevin went in the house to grab a shirt and shoes and rushed outside.

Landon was just about to get in his car when Kevin caught hold of his arm. Landon froze, not turning towards him at all as his emotions were currently on the surface and his temper was barely leashed. He concentrated hard to keep a lid on the power the king had unlocked for him.

"Don't go. I need to talk to you." Kevin stood close behind him. "I know how this looks but it's not what you think."

"Really? So you're telling me that you didn't go out with your friend and pick two chicks up, both of whom you brought home with you." Landon turned to face him slowly. "Because you have this desire not to come out, you went out last night and got stupid, didn't you?"

Kevin sighed and rubbed a hand down his face in frustration. "No, not that kind of stupid. I know it was dumb to let them come back with us but nothing happened. At least not on my end. I passed out."

Landon cocked his head to the side. "So, you got drunk and passed out, and I'm supposed to believe nothing happened. Tell me, do you remember all of last night?"

Kevin remained silent.

"Of course you don't. When you get drunk, you never remember anything. I'm pretty sure you and your boy had a nice little tag team thing going with the two chicks. I remember how you were before we were together. This is the type of thing you two used to do all the time. And since you were drunk and he doesn't know anything about us, you fell right back into the old habits."

"Babe..."

Landon snatched his arm free of Kevin's grip. "Go back and do what you were doing, Kevin."

Kevin grabbed his arm again. "No, I don't want us to end. And if you get in that car, I know that's what you're saying."

"Let go of my arm, Kevin," Landon warned.

"Not until you talk to me."

Landon turned and caught him off guard with a right hook to the jaw that knocked him clear off his feet. Kevin hit the pavement hard, and Johnny came running to his aid.

"What the hell is wrong with you?" He leaned down to check on Kevin, who was holding his jaw.

"He did something I didn't like, so I gave him what he deserved." Landon turned to get into his car.

This time it was Johnny that grabbed his arm. Johnny was a bit of a pretty boy, close to Landon's light brown skin color with light brown eyes and a low cut. He was a little heavier than Landon, though about the same height, and pretty toned in his own right. Like Kevin, he was in a pair of basketball shorts and a t-shirt, and right now had a frown on his face.

"Johnny, I suggest you get off my arm," Landon told him.

"Not until you tell me what the hell you hit him for," Johnny replied.

"I warned you." Landon turned and caught him with a right hook as well, although this time he aimed higher, catching Johnny in the side of the head. The effect was the same, although Johnny ended up with a glazed over look in his eyes. Landon looked down at them for a second before he finally got in his car and drove off. Later, he might regret hitting them. In that moment, it felt pretty good. At least he hadn't vaporized them both.

Landon went to work when he left Kevin's apartment and kept to himself. Working in a call center made that fairly easy, but normally Landon was a pretty social guy. Not on this day. He had too much on his mind now. And as he sat there, the object of his foul mood sent him a text.

I know I screwed up but can we please talk about this? And you don't have to just take my word for it. You can ask Johnny what happened.

Landon decided to ignore the message rather than respond. A few minutes later he got another one.

Don't ignore me. I love you and I don't want us to end. Please just talk to me.

Landon smirked. He found that hard to believe. The way he saw it something happened in that apartment last night between Kevin, Johnny, and those women. He knew Kevin always slept naked, and always threw on a pair of shorts when he got up. No matter what Kevin and Johnny said, there was no getting around what he thought. Kevin wasn't completely content with him alone. Against his better judgment, he decided to send a response.

Why do you insist on hounding me? I don't want to talk to you. I don't want to talk to Johnny. You and I both know what you did and I might respect you a bit more if you'd just admit it.

He put his phone away, hoping that would be the end of it. And it seemed to be the end, as he didn't hear from Kevin again before he went to lunch. On his lunch break, he went out to his car, intending to go get food, only to find Kevin leaning against it.

Damn, I do go to lunch the same time every day, Landon thought.

Still, he went to his car and Kevin straightened up.

"Look, I know you're mad and my jaw still hurts in case I might forget, but hear me out."

Landon gave him a blank stare. "You're holding me up from getting food and I'm hungry. Get the hell out of my way."

"Or what? You'll hit me again? Go ahead, Landon, hit me all you want. If that's what it takes to make this up to you then so be it."

Landon studied him. "Are you stupid? Even if I kick the shit out of you it's not going to make this situation go away."

"Then why did you hit me earlier, and why did you hit Johnny?" Kevin asked.

"I warned you both to let go of me. You chose not to. I punched you in the jaw and him in the side of the head. It was a reflex. The only reason you got off easier was because you're taller than me and it was easier to reach your jaw."

Kevin shook his head. "Look, I just want to talk. I want to apologize for whatever you think happened and whatever actually happened. I just want you to stay with me. I'll do whatever I can to make it up to you."

"There's nothing you can do, Kevin." Landon sighed. "If you really wanted me and wanted this to last, you'd have known better. Or at least you'd have been smart enough to try to hide it from me. Instead, you just didn't answer your phone at all and it made me suspicious. And you know what you and Johnny used to do. This makes me wonder if you've been doing the same thing all along and I just didn't know about it."

Kevin actually looked hurt. "Do you honestly think I'd have done that to you? That would imply that I'm just using you. Do you think this is just a passing fad for me?"

"I don't know anymore, Kevin. If it isn't, you have a horrible way of showing it."

"I would never intentionally do something like that to you. I told you before, I don't want to be like the rest of them."

"And yet you're actually worse than them," Landon said quietly.

Kevin's mouth dropped open in shock. Surely Landon hadn't actually said that to him.

"You're worse because you have never really been the faithful type before. You know everything I've gone through, every stupid bit of drama, and you swore never to put me through anything similar. And yet, here we are, in the same type of situation. The only difference is you chose to go back to women and each of my exes always slept with another man. You knew it all, and yet you couldn't change your ways. And you aren't man enough to admit that you can't change your ways and break off with me."

"Do you want me to break it off with you?" Kevin asked.

"I don't need you to," Landon answered. "I'm doing it for you. We're done, Kevin. Go back to what you know."

"What I know is you."

That almost moved Landon. But he shook his head.

"No, Kevin, we're done. Now move."

Kevin wanted to argue but Landon had a resigned look on his face that meant there would be no budging on this subject. He finally turned and walked off to his own car. Landon watched him for a few seconds, but finally got into his own car and sat there, forgetting about his desire for food.

"You really do like to overreact, don't you?"

Landon looked in his back seat to find the king sitting there. At least he'd dressed in clothes that wouldn't make him stand out so much in the mortal world. He was in a navy blue three-piece suit and tie, now lounging quite comfortably across the back seat with a grin on his face.

"You're watching me again. Shouldn't you be watching your son like this?" Landon asked, only a slight hint of irritation in his voice.

"I watch him very often. I've yet to make up my mind on this boy he's suddenly so interested in. I have a feeling that by the end I'll want to kill him. But in the meantime, you're overreacting. You really should give that poor boy a break."

Landon turned to face the king with a scowl. "Is giving love advice part of your job description?"

Damien chuckled. "It is when I choose to do so. That cold heart of yours is the reason you were reincarnated. You jump to conclusions far too quickly. In this case, you're wrong."

"You may be my king, but I know you like to toy with others. I'll handle this situation my way."

"Fine, suit yourself. I'm just a Magus king who can peer into the minds of mortals with frightening ease. I'll be needing to see my son soon. You should make that happen."

Landon rolled his eyes. "He has no idea that I know you or am connected to you in any way. How precisely do you expect me to pull off a meeting with you?"

"Just figure out somewhere for us to run into each other. It's not like I'm an unknown factor for him."

"You're a barely known factor and he resents you for it. Do you have any idea what he's been through?"

Damien frowned. "Oh, I know exactly what happened while I was caught up in the affairs of Avalon. Trust me, those responsible are not enjoying their lives at this moment."

"Yeah, well deep down, Brian blames you for it. You weren't there and he resents you for it. You're still not there, in his eyes."

"One day, he'll understand that the world is not black and white. It's not entirely my choice. The point is, I would like to see him away from his home and I cannot contact his mother."

Landon sighed. "I'll arrange it within the next few days. At some point, we have to tell him who he really is."

"Soon enough, he'll know." Damien vanished.

Chapter Nine

Landon left his phone off for the rest of his shift, just to get some time to get his mind off of Kevin and their situation. Throwing himself into his work for the next four hours certainly didn't leave him any time to reflect on his love life. When he left work and got into his car, he turned his phone back on and discovered he had a voicemail waiting on him. He sighed, and checked it anyway. Surprisingly, it was Brian, not Kevin.

"Dude, where are you? Why is your phone off? I really needed you and your phone is off. I know you're at work but your phone is never off. Call me as soon as you get this."

Landon swore under his breath and quickly called Brian. Brian picked up on the third ring.

"Where the hell are you?" Brian demanded.

"I just got off work," Landon answered. "What's wrong, kid?"

"Can you come get me? I really need you right now."

"Where are you?" Landon asked.

"I'm at Kevin's house. He came to get me since you turned your phone off."

"You've got to be fucking kidding me," Landon muttered.

"What?"

"Don't worry about it, I'm on my way." Landon hung up and started his car. It was just his luck that Kevin came through for Brian today.

Landon got out of his car and walked up to Kevin's door. Before he could knock, Kevin opened the door.

"Just to forewarn you, today was not a good day for him," Kevin told him. "Try not to rage when you see him. He just needs you to comfort him right now."

Landon scowled. "I don't like the sound of that."

"Trust me, when you see him, you'll understand. It was all I could do not to go to jail for this crap." Kevin stepped aside to let him in.

Brian was sitting on the futon, curled up in a ball. He looked up as Landon came in, and what Landon saw made him see red. Kevin closed the door behind him and put a hand on his shoulder. Landon looked back at him and Kevin simply looked into his eyes. Landon exhaled and walked forward, sitting next to Brian, who immediately leaned in to him and wrapped his arms around him. Landon looked down at him and took note of his split lip and a noticeable black eye. Brian buried his face in Landon's chest and clearly couldn't fight the urge to cry. A sob wracked his entire body and Landon simply held him. Kevin left the room to give them time alone.

When Brian stopped, Landon finally spoke.

"What happened?" he asked.

"Mom's husband decided it was a good idea to hit me today," Brian answered.

"Give me the whole story, so that I know *exactly* why I'm breaking my foot off in his ass."

"I came home from school and there were dishes in the sink. I went to my room, and he called me out and told me to wash them. I told him no because I didn't use any of them. I haven't been home all day. His solution to it was this."

"Where was your mother?"

"She was at work. He was drunk, again."

Landon kept his face blank. "Have you talked to her since you got here?"

"Yeah, she knows."

Landon lifted Brian's face up to look him in the eye. "I'm sorry I wasn't there for you today. I wasn't thinking straight when I turned my phone off. It's no excuse really. What I've got going on is nothing compared to this."

"I'm fine. It looks worse than it is." Brian tried to smile but didn't really succeed at it.

"I don't care if it does. I'm going to have some words with your stepfather."

Brian leaned back and took a deep breath. "Don't do anything crazy."

"I'm not, and you're not going back there. We'll go get you some clothes and then you're staying with me."

"What about my mom?" Brian asked. "I don't know if she'll go along with this."

Landon's face hardened. "Oh, she'll go along with it. Especially after I'm done. Now wait here."

He stood up and went into Kevin's bedroom. Kevin was sitting on the bed and looked over when he came in.

"Don't thank me. It was nothing," he told him.

"No, that means a lot to me," Landon replied. "We're not together, but you still went and got him out of there for me."

Kevin looked him in the eyes. "The two of us not being together has nothing to do with him. He needed someone and it's my fault he couldn't get to you."

Landon sighed. "You could have ignored him but you didn't. That's all that really matters to me."

"Do you want me to go with you when you go to get his things?" Kevin asked.

"No, but thanks. I've got it from here." Landon turned and left the room.

"Are you sure about this? We could wait until he's not there to go get my things." Brian was clearly afraid to re-enter his home.

"If you want, call your mom, and have her gather some stuff for you, but we're going there tonight. And there's no need to worry about him. I've got a surprise for him."

Landon parked in front of Brian's house and told him to go to the door. Brian did so reluctantly as Landon opened his trunk and reached inside. He left the lock box inside. He didn't need what was in it for this. Instead he pulled out a pair of gloves used for mixed martial arts training and fighting. He slipped them on his hands and walked up to the door as Brian's mother opened it to let her son in.

Brian's mother, Denise, was a short, light skinned woman with long brownish blonde hair and light brown eyes. She was a little heavier set, but overall a very pretty woman with a fairly large rack that was immediately noticeable.

"Where is he, Denise?" Landon asked her.

"Downstairs in the family room playing his game, as usual." Denise looked at his hands. "Clearly, there's no stopping you this time."

"Nope." Landon stepped into the house and headed for the basement. Brian followed, mostly because his bedroom was there, but also out of fear of what Landon had planned. At the bottom of the stairs, Landon pointed to Brian's room and Brian broke off to gather his things. Landon went into the family room across the short hall.

There in a recliner sat Brian's stepfather, Paul. He was a larger man, taller than Landon by a few inches. He was fat, to be quite blunt, and out of shape. He was slightly darker in skin tone than Landon and his head was shaved. Clearly, he used to be in shape, but had let himself go. Either way, it didn't matter to Landon.

"Yo, big man, I've got a bone to pick with you."

"What is...." Paul was cut off when Landon's fist met his face. His teeth rattled and he fell to the side slightly. Landon in turn flipped his chair over to dump him on the thinly carpeted floor.

"Come on, big guy. Let's see you hit me like you hit Brian earlier." Landon kicked him hard in the spine. "Get up and show me what you've got."

Paul began to push himself up on all fours and Landon kicked him in the ribs this time, getting him to emit a loud groan. Landon looked around and spotted the Xbox the larger man had been playing. He picked it up and yanked the cords free, then bashed Paul across the head with it. The plastic electronic device cracked with ease across the larger man's head and he cried out this time in pain. The plastic cut into his head and blood began to pour from the scratches. Landon held the Xbox up and examined it.

"That's not good enough." Landon hit him again with the object again and again, stopping only when it was suitably broken. Then he tossed it and knelt beside him.

Paul groaned low again, still conscious.

"Oh, so that didn't take you out? Good, now my fists can do the rest."

With that said, Landon started swinging, striking the larger man repeatedly in the face. He felt quite satisfied when he felt Paul's nose break and even more when he knocked several of his teeth loose. He let up finally and stood up, wiping a bit of sweat from his brow.

"Now, while you're conscious, let's get a few things straight. First off, I've been waiting to do that for years. The only thing saving your ass this long has been your wife. But today, you got stupid. You put your hands on what's mine, fat ass. I have a problem with useless, whiny, pathetic fucks like you. You don't work, you sit down here and play your little video games all day long. Your wife works and pays all the bills, and now Brian helps out. He goes to school all day, gets off, comes home for a few minutes and then goes to work to pay the bills your fat ass is supposed to pay. For you to sit here and put your hands on him like you're some kind of big man kind of pisses me off. So, here's what's going to happen. Tonight, Brian is going home with me. Whenever he wants to come home, he will. And guess what? If you're still here, which would supremely piss me off, you're never going to lay a hand on him again. You're not even going to look at him funny. If you so much as breathe in his direction, I'll be back. And it'll cost you way more than your Xbox and the trip you'll be making to the hospital when I'm done here."

Another groan let him know that Paul heard at least the last line. He tried to move and Landon kicked him hard in the side of the head. Paul rolled over from the force of the kick and wound up lying on his back, his eyes rolling back into his head before he finally passed out. Just for good measure, Landon turned the chair over on top of him before he left the family room.

Brian had finished gathering what he needed.

"Let's go." Landon took his hand and led him up the stairs. He didn't stop until they reached the door, where Denise was waiting.

"So what now?" she asked.

"That's on you, Denise," Landon answered. "I'm taking Brian until he's ready to come back. If fat ass is still here, you'll be seeing a lot more of me. I'm not kidding anymore, Denise. I will beat the hell out of him again and again if he's still around. I can't tell you what to do about your marriage, but I can make damn sure this kid feels safe. And if ever he comes to me looking like this again, your husband is going to bleed out slowly and never be found again."

With that, he pushed Brian out of the door and they headed to the car. Once inside, Brian looked at Landon for several seconds.

"What is it?" Landon asked him.

"I heard all the noise in there and I just can't believe you did that," Brian answered quietly.

"There's a lot more to me than meets the eye, kid. I have a thing about bullies. They piss me off and I like to kick the crap out of them. Most importantly, I don't want to see you hurt again. You've been through enough in life without him deciding to take his failures as a man out on you."

"Still, that was kind of brutal."

Landon smirked. "I never said I fight fair. I gave him what he deserved. And maybe now he'll at least try to do something with himself since he doesn't have the Xbox to play all day. Maybe I should have broken the computer too."

"Let's not take things overboard. The computer is mine."

Landon shrugged and started the car. "It doesn't matter. You're staying with me now. Let's go get food."

Chapter Ten

The next day Landon took Brian to school before going on with his usual day. He gave Brian a spare key to his apartment so that he could get in after school and went to work as usual. When he got off, he decided to hit the gym. Brian asked to go, so he stopped to get him first, though not before letting the king know where they'd be. Normally, he'd have music on for his work out, but since Brian was working out alongside him, he decided not to. Besides, Brian wanted to talk.

They stepped on the treadmills to start off with a walk.

"So, what's going on with you and Kevin?" Brian asked.

Landon sighed. "Do we really have to go into this?"

"Yeah we do. You guys were acting weird yesterday. And your phone hasn't gone off once today since you got off work. I almost feel like I shouldn't have called him to come get me yesterday."

Landon gave him a sharp look. "No, you were right to call him when you couldn't get me. What goes on between me and him doesn't have to affect you. He and I aren't together, but if you need help and he's willing to do it, go for it."

"But why aren't you together?"

Landon looked away. "It's not an easy thing for me to talk about, Brian. But let's just say he's not that different from the exes I had before him."

Brian was quiet for several seconds. "So he cheated on you?"

"As far as I'm concerned, yes," Landon answered.

"So there's a possibility he didn't?"

Landon scowled. "He says he didn't, but don't they all? Look, I know how he was before. I know the things he did before me. And when I went to his house yesterday morning, I saw the signs that he'd gone back to his old ways. His best friend was there with two chicks."

Brian gave him a confused look.

"They used to find two chicks and do them in the same room together. And they've shared the same chick before too," Landon explained.

"But, does that mean he did it this time?"

Landon said nothing, merely continued to walk on the treadmill. Brian, however, wasn't finished.

"Come on, bro, you know Kevin better than that. You know he wouldn't hurt you for the world. Isn't it possible that he let Johnny bring the girls over but he didn't do anything with them?"

Landon rolled his eyes. "I know Kevin all too well. That's why it's more likely that he did it than not. Look, Brian, I know you wanted me and Kevin to work. I wanted us to work more than anyone. But he's a closet case that has no intention of ever coming out. So to keep Johnny from figuring out that he likes men, yes, I believe he would sleep with those women. He may have been drunk, and he can try to blame the decision on that, but the fact is, on some level, he wanted to do it."

"I still think he wouldn't have done it," Brian pressed.

"Well, it's nice that you like him enough to want to believe that. Call me jaded, but I've been waiting for it to happen for months. And now I'm wondering if this is the first time it's happened."

Brian knew when he was beating his head against a brick wall, and he could do without the headache.

"I need to use the bathroom. I'll be back." He stopped the treadmill and walked off.

Landon kept walking, though he watched Brian go into the bathroom. He was getting a bit paranoid about his little brother figure.

"The boy takes after me a lot."

Landon wasn't surprised that the king was now on the treadmill next to him. At least he'd changed into sweatpants and a t-shirt to match normal gym attire.

"He's about to meddle, isn't he?" Landon asked.

"Oh yes, and you can't really be angry about it. Someone has to do it. You're letting previous hurts affect your judgment."

"Well unfortunately I'm not really capable of reading minds. You bound most of my powers and you haven't released that one," Landon told him bitterly.

Damien shrugged. "It was necessary to reincarnate you into this life. You have much to learn about humanity. I need you as a complete warrior."

"I'm little more than human as it is. I was born to a mortal mother and father. I age like a human. I have no memory of my life as your warrior. The only thing that has set me apart for most of my life is the strength and speed I have that seems to be growing."

Damien smiled. "Oh yes, these little gym excursions are barely even necessary. I think you do them out of habit."

"It'll help Brian too, when his powers are released and his form alters like we all do."

"I did unlock quite a bit of your power, though the power you naturally possessed in your previous life is vast. I must admit even I never knew the extent of it. You have the ability to read minds. You simply have to figure out how to use it."

Landon scowled. "You couldn't have mentioned that? I don't know how to use most of this power you released."

"Your body will remember in time. And you will need them soon enough."

Landon glanced at the king. "What's headed my way?"

"You have some of your memories, don't you?" Damien asked.

"Not as much as I'd like, but some particularly traumatic ones surface in my nightmares."

"Well, sometimes nightmares become reality," the king said cryptically.

In the bathroom, Brian pulled out his cell phone. Landon was going to hit the roof if he found out what he was doing. Still, he was going to deal with his friend's temper. He dialed the number and waited for an answer.

"What's up, kid?" Kevin asked when he answered the phone.

"Are you busy?"

"Nah, I'm just at home. Why?"

"Me and Landon are at the gym. I think you should come by."

Kevin let out a breath. "I don't think that would be smart. Landon doesn't want to see me right now."

Brian scoffed at that. "Yes he does. He just doesn't want to admit it."

"You don't know the whole story."

"Yes, I do. He just told me. And I know my friend. He wants to see you but he's hurt. You've got to stay on him. You didn't do anything, did you?"

Kevin stayed silent.

"Did you?" Brian pressed.

"No, I didn't, but you know how it looks. I can't blame him for not believing me. And if it were anyone but him, I'd have been lying if I said I hadn't done it. But there's no way to make him believe me. I even offered to have Johnny talk to him but Landon doesn't want to hear anything from me. You know how he gets when he makes up his mind."

"Yeah, and I know if you stay on him long enough he'll listen to you and he'll see it the way I do."

Kevin couldn't help but smile, even though Brian couldn't see it. "I'm glad you believe me. But I know Landon just as well as you do. And he has this thing about being cheated on. Once he gets it in his mind that someone cheated then that's all there is to it."

"So you won't come?" Brian asked.

Kevin thought for a few seconds. "I'll try it this time. But don't expect him to be forgiving. If he even talks to me, I'll be surprised."

Brian hung up and went back out to join Landon, who had moved to one of the many weight machines. Landon stopped as he approached.

"Are you ok?" Landon asked.

"I'm fine," Brian responded, perhaps a bit too quickly.

Landon narrowed his eyes at him. "You're up to something."

"No, I'm not," Brian lied.

"You're lying," Landon replied. "But I'll let it go for now. Anyway, how was school?"

Brian let him start on the machine again before responding. "I got some questions about my eye and my lip. I told the truth, and I told them I'm staying with you now."

"Did they call your mom?" Landon asked.

"Yeah, they called her but I didn't stay around long enough to find out what was said."

"Have you talked to her?"

"She called to check on me when I got out of school."

The two fell silent. Brian decided to start working out on another machine next to Landon, and they were joined by the king. Landon was doing a full body workout and Brian was just trying to keep up. Damien found it all a bit too easy but it was time with his son, time he so rarely had anymore. As they stopped to take a break, Kevin walked into the gym. Landon stiffened and Brian was thankful that he didn't have to hold his gaze while Damien chuckled softly. Kevin stopped at the water fountain first for a drink before hitting the treadmill for the warm up. Landon scowled and walked off in another direction, purposely avoiding him. Brian, however, went over to stand in front of Kevin's treadmill.

"Why didn't you go talk to him?" he demanded.

"I didn't see you, and besides, Landon and I start our workouts the same way," Kevin answered. "If I'd gone searching for him, he'd have figured out that I only came tonight because you told me he was here. I figured I'd at least start off here and then find you guys."

Brian rolled his eyes. "You two are such big babies. You love each other so work it out already."

"It takes more than love to keep a relationship together. Landon doesn't trust me and I can't even say that I blame him. We've known each other for so long. He knows all the dirt I used to do, all the lies I used to tell, and the games I used to play. What sucks is that I know he loves me with all his heart, and I love him, but he was just waiting for me to mess up."

"You know him pretty well too," Brian said quietly.

"Yeah, I do. And I know I'll never find another like him. He's a little rough around the edges and has a mean right hook, but I want him."

Brian looked over to see Landon heading to the free weights. "Why don't you go spot him then? Gives you a reason to talk."

Kevin stopped the treadmill and headed towards Landon.

"I love the way you meddle, son," Damien told the younger male as he came to stand behind him.

Brian didn't seem surprised. His father had always seemed to appear out of nowhere.

"Someone had to do something so they'd get it together."

"Yes, I suppose they did. Speaking of which, I hear you have someone special in your life. We should talk about him."

Brian raised an eyebrow. "Him? What are you talking about?"

Damien laughed. "Did you think your mother and I were clueless? We know your preferences and are perfectly fine with them."

"I didn't know you and Mom talked that much."

"Oh yes, even when I can't get a hold of you, I stay in some form of contact with your mother to check on you. So, who's the boy and when do I get to meet him and instill the fear of hell in him?" Damien grinned, the glamour that dulled his beauty shimmering for a split second. There was nothing like an overprotective Magus King.

Landon frowned at Kevin when he approached but nonetheless lay across the bench. Kevin stood behind him as he lifted the bar to begin.

"I know you're still mad at me, but I miss you already," Kevin told him.

Landon merely grunted but said nothing.

"And I know you're not going to talk to me, but since you're here I'm guessing you're willing to listen. You may not believe it, but I really didn't do anything with them."

Landon held the bar up and Kevin took it from him, setting it back in place. Landon sat up and turned to look at him.

"Why should I believe you?" Landon asked.

"I told you to ask Johnny. He's got no reason to lie to you. And I'm having this conversation with you out loud in public. I'd never have done this before, and I'd never do it for anyone but you."

"That proves nothing to me Kevin. As far as I'm concerned, Johnny would lie for you if you asked him to."

"I've never asked him to lie for me any more than I asked you to lie for me before we got together. I don't need anyone to lie for me. I told him about us yesterday. I had to explain why you knocked the hell out of me."

Landon actually laughed. "That had to have been an entertaining conversation. But it doesn't change anything." He stood to leave.

"Landon." Kevin didn't touch him this time, having learned the day before where that would get him.

Landon stopped. "Kevin, we need space. Maybe after I have time to think about it I can accept what you're saying. But right now, I don't believe it. I believe what it looked like. What I saw hurt, Kevin, and you of all people know why it hurt. So just leave me alone."

"I can't do that. I know you. I know if I let you sit and think then you'll just get madder. I want you to believe me and forgive me for being dumb enough to let it look like it did. I don't want you to leave me alone completely. If you can't move past it, I at least want to remain friends."

Landon looked back at him. "I make you no promises, but this one time, I'm telling you, leave me alone. I'll talk to you when I'm good and ready to deal with this."

He walked off, leaving Kevin staring after him.

Chapter Eleven

L andon pulled up to his own apartment to a surprise. Johnny was waiting outside his door.

"What do you want Johnny?" he asked irritably.

"I need to talk to you about Kevin," Johnny replied.

"What's there to talk about? I already talked to him."

"But you don't believe him."

Landon gave him a dull stare. "I know his history, and I know yours. I see no reason for me to believe him."

"Look, just give me a little time to explain things to you and then I'll leave you alone."

Landon sighed. "Fine, come inside and say what you have to say."

He opened the door and the two stepped inside. Landon tossed his keys on an end table in the living room and sat down in an armchair. Johnny sat down on the sofa.

"Look, I didn't know about the two of you or I wouldn't have brought the girls back to his place. He never told me."

"Of course, he didn't. You're a homophobe. Why would he have told you?" Landon questioned.

"I'm his best friend. I'm not going to turn on him for being who he is. And I'm not a homophobe. I just don't want a gay dude hitting on me."

Landon rolled his eyes. "You're not that attractive to be honest, and you're an asshole, which makes you downright ugly. I doubt very seriously any gay male would waste their time hitting on you."

Johnny sucked in his breath. "Damn, that was mean."

"Since when have I ever been nice?" Landon asked. "I believe in being honest. Straight men get uneasy for the stupidest reasons. And really, is it that you don't want the dude to hit on you, or that you're afraid of your own response to a guy hitting on you?"

Johnny scowled at him. "Dude, I'm not gay."

"Keep telling yourself that." Landon leaned forward. "Ask yourself this, though. If you're not gay, why did you and Kevin always bang these broads in the same room? Why did you tag team some of them? Taking turns, I could sort of understand. But y'all went in at the same time on some of them. I kind of wonder, was one on bottom while the chick was in the middle and the other on the top? Did you ever reach up and grab the other's ass to make the other fuck her harder? Or how about when it comes time for one of you to nut? Do you know tricks to make the other nut at the same time?"

Johnny's face turned red. "Shut up."

"I'm just asking out of curiosity." Landon sat back. "And for the record, I already know the answer to those questions. So, you understand why I don't believe this little story that you tagged both broads alone."

"Look, I'm not the best dude around. But I wouldn't come between my boy and what makes him happy. He's miserable right now. He doesn't do anything but work and come home. Nothing I can do will cheer him up. He just wants you."

"He has a fucked up way of showing it," Landon replied.

"Didn't he come talk to you the other day?" Johnny asked.

"Yeah, so?"

"Couldn't you see how he was doing?" Johnny demanded. "You know him almost as well as I do, right? You know full well he never did that for a single broad. He didn't have to and didn't want to. He's actually begging you."

"Is that supposed to mean something special to me?" Landon actually laughed. "That doesn't tell me that he didn't do anything wrong. To me, it means he's guilty."

Johnny ran a hand down his face in frustration. "I promise you that he didn't do anything. He passed out when we got to the house. He was completely drunk."

"Did he wake up at any point after he passed out?" Landon asked.

"No, he stripped down to his shorts before he passed out. He was hot. Then he slept until you got there."

"Why did he look guilty when he opened the door then?" Landon demanded.

"He knew what you would think. Even I can admit it looks bad but seriously, this was all me. Just talk to him again, please? I hate to see him like this."

Landon looked at him for a few seconds, thinking over it. "I'll talk to him soon enough. But I'm not making any promises. In the event I was to take him back, if something like this happens again, I'm kicking your ass. No questions asked and no conversation. My foot meets your ass immediately upon discovery."

Johnny rubbed his jaw. "I haven't forgotten the other day either. I owe you for that."

Landon smirked. "Good luck collecting on that. Now, are you finished?"

Johnny stood up. "Yeah. But seriously, don't leave my boy hanging."

Landon waved him off and watched him walk out. It would seem that there was no avoiding this Kevin situation, no matter what he did.

Chapter Twelve

L andon avoided Kevin for weeks. Brian continued to stay with him and every so often would try to get him to call Kevin over. Landon refused each time. Kevin wouldn't come to the gym when Brian asked either. He knew why the boy was asking, and there was no point. Landon didn't do anything he didn't want to do.

To be honest, the distance was getting to Landon as well. He'd been without sex since the breakup. Landon needed sex, and he needed good sex. It was annoying that he couldn't work up the will to find another guy for it. He wanted Kevin, but it would be rather misleading to call him solely to get his rocks off.

On his way home, he got a call from Brian.

"Hey, I'm going to stay out a little late tonight. I've got a date."

Landon snorted. "A date with the mystery man I've yet to meet. I think he should pick you up from the house and come inside to meet me."

"We're already out," Brian replied.

"All right, fine. But be home at a reasonable hour."

"Define reasonable."

"Midnight, I guess."

"Ok."

Brian hung up. Landon sighed and pulled into his parking lot. As he reached his door, he found yet another surprise.

"What are you doing here, Kevin?"

Kevin kept his face blank. "I'm tired of this. Open the door and let's go inside."

Landon raised an eyebrow. "What the hell got into you?"

"Over a month of no sex makes me irritable. Now open the damn door."

Landon bit his lip to keep from laughing and opened the door, letting Kevin go inside first. As soon as he closed the door and turned around, Kevin pinned him against the door and took his mouth forcefully. Landon made a slight sound of protest and shoved him back.

"What the hell are you doing?" he demanded.

"Look, you may not want to talk, but I have it on good authority you haven't had sex either. And I know you. I don't care what you think of me right now. We're going to solve this issue." He reached out and pulled Landon towards him and the two fell back onto the couch, with Landon on top of him.

"Wait a minute, this is not helping..." Landon started.

Kevin put a hand over his mouth. "Shut it. This is going to happen whether you like it or not."

Landon glared down at him but said nothing, which was only because Kevin still had his hand over his mouth.

"You have a choice, bed or couch," Kevin told him as he removed his hand.

"Neither, you jackass. We're not screwing."

Kevin flipped their positions. "Your mouth says no but your body says yes."

Landon was quite clearly aroused, but damned if he'd let it go to his head. "We're still not screwing."

"Really? Let's just see about that." Kevin rose up and pulled Landon up with him, this time throwing him over his shoulder and carrying him to the bedroom. Landon squirmed until Kevin threw him on the bed.

"You do realize I'm going to hurt you for this, right?" he asked rudely.

"Do whatever you have to, but I'm tired of waiting on you." Kevin started removing his clothes. "You love me and I love you. You've been torturing us both for weeks. I'm just doing what you want to do and won't." He stood fully naked and looked down at Landon. "You want it. I know you do. You can hate me later but we need this right now."

Landon bit the inside of his mouth to keep his expression blank. Kevin's body had always been a turn on. And all of him was standing at attention. Landon was unable to move. He was torn. Part of him reminded him that they weren't together and that doing this would only add to Kevin's attachment. But the other part didn't give a damn. Kevin didn't wait, however. He knew where Landon kept the things he needed for this to happen, and he grabbed them quickly. He unfastened Landon's pants for him and pulled them off, along with his boxers.

Resigned, Landon sat up enough to pull off his shirt. As he was doing so, Kevin knelt down and took him into his mouth. Landon hissed and his hands automatically went to Kevin's head to guide him. Kevin moaned, sending a slight vibration through him as he continued to work him. Landon closed his eyes and leaned back to enjoy, but a few moments later, Kevin stopped. Landon opened his eyes again to find Kevin straddling him.

"Wait, is this really what you want?" he asked.

Kevin smirked. "If I didn't want it, I wouldn't do it. I want you, and I want to make sure you enjoy this."

He positioned himself just above Landon after applying lube, and slowly slid down. When he was about halfway down, Landon surged up, entering him the rest of the way. Kevin grunted and leaned down, taking his lips again as he began to ride. He moved slowly at first so that he wouldn't break their kiss. Landon wrapped his arms around him, running his hands up and down his back as he simply had to touch him all over. Kevin's thick erection rode up Landon's abdomen and as Kevin pulled away just slightly to increase his speed, Landon watched his member slide up and down. Kevin sat up and moved even faster, riding him hard and his erection sprang up, no longer resting on Landon's stomach. He was turned on. Landon could feel him getting close. His balls tightened and he clamped down on Landon. He was trying to hold off, trying to wait for Landon.

"Do it," Landon whispered.

Kevin moved faster and finally he couldn't hold back anymore. He came with a loud moan, spraying all over Landon's chest and stomach. Landon reached up and pulled him down to take his lips again, and then pumped up into him hard and fast. Kevin moaned repeatedly as Landon kept going, pumping up from under him until finally he cried out as he came as well. They broke the kiss and Kevin lay on top of him for a few seconds before rolling off him to lie on the bed next to him. For several moments, the two lay staring at the ceiling.

"So what now?" Kevin finally asked.

Landon snorted. "You were so forceful before. You tell me."

Kevin sighed. "You still love me and I still love you. I want you back. What will it take for us to get back together?"

"I don't trust you, so the only way to work this is to open the relationship."

Kevin sat up and stared at him. "Are you serious?"

"Yeah, I am."

"So you want to sleep around now?"

Landon shrugged. "More like I don't trust you not to sleep around. You can choose whether or not you actually do it but this way I don't have to stress it if you do."

Kevin flopped back down on the bed. "I can't believe this. You can't just turn off your emotions like that. I know you."

"Do you really?" Landon asked. "I can turn off all emotion if I so choose. I may love you, but I'm practical. If I'm not enough for you but you're determined to be with me in some way, then this is the best I can offer you."

"I can't agree to that. I want you and I don't want you with anyone else. I can't believe you would even ask me that."

Landon rolled his eyes. "Stop getting emotional. I never said I'd make use of it either. It just makes situations like this much easier."

"No it doesn't. Not for me. If we do this, I know you'll be messing around. It's a free pass for you to get some variety."

"Last I checked, you're the one that always needed variety, not me," Landon argued.

Kevin glared at him. "Not with you. I don't need anyone but you. What can I do to make you see that?"

"Agree to my terms," Landon told him. "Maybe if you don't mess around we can go back to normal."

Kevin remained silent as he thought it over. In the end, he had no choice but to agree.

"Fine, I'll agree to this. But I'm not going to act like we're just screwing. We're together in my mind, so I'm going to act like you're mine."

"Whatever you say guy. Just don't be surprised when I put you back in your place." Landon rolled over onto his side to catch a nap.

Kevin rolled with him and threw an arm around him. Landon merely grunted and allowed himself to drift off. The problem was solved for now, although he wondered if he should have fought against Kevin harder.

Chapter Thirteen

Several weeks went by and Landon came home late one evening. School was out for the summer and things had been going well. What he found pissed him off immediately, as Brian was sitting alone crying on the couch.

"What the hell?" he swore under his breath as he sat next to the boy.

Brian immediately leaned into him and sobbed. Clearly, this wasn't the time for words and Landon simply held him until he stopped. His natural urge to soothe the younger male manifested in his power, as he soon noticed energy flowing from him into Brian and the sobs soon quieted.

"What in the blue hell happened and who do I get to kill?" Landon asked with quiet anger.

"I just feel stupid. All this time I've been dating Leon and he's just been looking for someone else. And now he found him and slept with him. He called me earlier and told me about it like it was just normal." Brian laughed humorlessly. "Seriously, he picked up the phone and just starts telling me all about how he hooked up with this guy. And when I spoke up it was almost like it caught him off guard. So after telling me all of the sordid details of his affair, he tells me we should just be friends. After months of talking to him and we've been out on dates and instead of being man enough to tell me before he slept with the guy, he went out and fucked him, then came home and told me about it. Oh, and get this. The bastard is in Texas and neglected to tell me that too. I didn't mean shit to him."

"I hate to say it like this, but this type of thing happens. Leon is someone you should learn from and move away from. You don't want him as a friend either if this is how he treats you." Landon continued to hold him while rubbing his shoulder. "You loved that boy, and any idiot could see it. You were so happy when you were around him or had been around him. He's the worst type of person to do this to you. In the end it's your choice, but you really shouldn't deal with it."

"Ugh, and I was so patient with him. He was a virgin when I met him. I was waiting for him, determined to let him decide when he was ready and then be his first. I feel like he's been lying to me all along. Maybe he wasn't a virgin. Maybe this is just the latest in the list of guys he's been with and he lost track of who he was actually screwing, so he called me to tell me about this one, forgetting that we've been dating."

"Okay, start over and tell me everything from the beginning. Because right now I want to hunt him down and hang him over the Chain of Rocks Bridge by his toes with twenty pound weights tied to his arms."

Brian laughed with a little bit of actual humor this time. "I love you."

Landon snorted. "I know. Now explain it all, from the beginning of the relationship until now."

"Well, you know I had a crush on him for a while before I finally approached him and we exchanged numbers. We talked a lot in the beginning. He listened when I was going through all the things with Paul and he made me feel better. He was the whole reason I smiled." Brian glanced at him. "Other than the times I could hang out with you."

Landon smiled. "I'm not offended. You were in love. I'm like your older brother figure. It's cool."

Brian nodded and continued. "So it didn't take long for me to make my intentions clear. I wanted him and only him. I knew he was a virgin and I was willing to go without sex until he was ready. I told him this. I even told him I wanted him to be the first to, you know, do me. Whenever he was ready, I'd be ready for him. And you know that was a big step for me. We talked every day that we didn't see each other. And those few dates we went on were his idea. We stayed up late a lot of nights talking. I wouldn't get off the phone until I was literally on the verge of sleep. You saw how often we were together. I guess all along he was just telling me things I want to hear. He acted like we were together. The calls, the texts, everything. I met a couple of his friends. And then today, he calls me with this. Now, he wants to just be friends, after he's met someone else. I didn't even know he was looking for anyone else. I thought everything was going fine."

"So, out of the blue, he comes up with this new guy? What's the new guy's name?" Landon asked.

"He said his name is Matt," Brian answered. "Apparently they've been talking for a while. Months even. I don't even know how that's possible."

Landon sighed. "Isn't Leon older than you?"

"Yeah, he just graduated."

"Does he work?"

Brian raised an eyebrow in question but still responded. "Yeah."

"Does he have a set schedule?"

"No," Brian answered cautiously.

"Clearly he was talking to the guy then, and probably using that as an excuse to go see him as well. Honestly, you shouldn't bother trying to wrap your head around it. No matter how many times you try, you'll never understand this situation. You'll never know why, no matter what he tells you. Even if he told you the truth, he lied to you about everything else so you wouldn't believe him. This will only stress you out more than you already are and it makes the pain worse. You just have to let him go. Believe me, even if he comes back to you, this situation will always stick in your mind. Just let him go."

Brian sighed and lay back against him. Neither of the two spoke for a while. Until Brian's phone rang. He sighed as he looked at the caller ID.

"It's Leon isn't it?" Landon asked.

"Yeah, it's him."

Landon took the phone from him and hit the ignore button, then turned the phone off and took the battery out.

"Why did you do that?" Brian asked.

"Because he's going to keep calling and the more he calls the more likely you are to answer. Once you answer he's going to apologize and tell you a whole bunch of bullshit to make you forgive him. And I'm sorry but things will only get worse from here if you take him back. I'd rather not see you go through that." Landon handed him the phone without a battery. "I'll give you the battery back tomorrow. Now go get some sleep."

"Don't you sound downright fatherly?" Brian scowled as he stood and went to prepare for bed.

Landon smirked and watched him walk off. He looked at the battery in his hand, a feeling of dread deep in his soul. In the end, he couldn't stop Brian from doing what he wanted, and once Brian got that battery back, Landon knew he would answer Leon's calls. After all, it's what he'd have done at that age as well.

"So, I get to kill the boy now, right?"

Landon wasn't surprised to find the king had popped in yet again unannounced. "I'm fairly certain Brian will wonder why the hell you're here and how you got in here."

"He can't hear us. I'm not a complete idiot."

"No need to kill anyone just because it's his first heartbreak," Landon told him. "Besides, the boy is human. We're not supposed to kill them unless it's in self-defense."

Damien grunted. "I made the damn laws. I know how to follow them. But it would make me immensely happy to see the boy suffer for his heartless treatment of my prince. My son has a big destiny ahead of him. I'd hate for some half-wit to ruin it."

"He'll be fine if he leaves the boy alone," Landon assured the king.

"Brian has more going on than you know of, Landon. Keep a closer watch over him. If anything happens to my son I will have that human in my dungeons along with the last stupid little human that hurt my boy."

"Why isn't Paul in that dungeon exactly?"

Damien scowled. "Because Denise is an imbecile and has some form of feelings for the wretched creature. But no matter. You can kill him if he harms my child again. I demand that you do so."

"Gladly, but why are you here?" Landon asked.

"There's nothing more important to me than my son's health and happiness. His distress reached me in Avalon. Since I couldn't pop in and ask him myself, I had to wait for you."

"That's it?"

"Oh no, you and I will be taking a brief trip. Don't worry, it won't keep you from your mortal world obligations. But it's about time for you to work on mastering the power I've released in you. There are stirrings in Avalon and I need you to be the warrior I knew before." The king extended his hand. "Take my hand."

Landon did so and was blinded by a flash of green light.

Chapter Fourteen

Brian got his battery back the next morning and went to work at the job he'd gotten right before school ended at Sonic, the fast food restaurant. Surprisingly, it didn't go off at all during the day. Sure, Leon had sent him loads of text messages trying to get him to answer the phone and begging him to call that day. Brian deleted them all. His chest actually hurt every time he thought about Leon. His mind was barely on his work. He'd been through a lot in his life but none of it hurt like this. No matter what Landon said, he kept trying to figure out where it all went wrong. When had Leon lost interest? Was he so unapproachable that Leon just couldn't tell him earlier that they were done? Or was Leon just that type of jerk? He had so many questions and no real way to answer them.

When his shift was at its end, he didn't even notice. It wasn't until a coworker said something to him that he left. Landon was at work so he'd be catching the bus home. That was fine. He loved Landon more than just about anyone, but he didn't want to be around him now. Landon was the overprotective type, and while that was nice most times, he couldn't deal with it right now. He needed the alone time to think.

Of course, his phone went off as he was about to leave out of the door. It was Leon. He debated on whether to send him to voicemail again or not, but in the end he caved and answered.

"What do you want?" he demanded much more harshly than he expected.

"We need to talk in person. I'm waiting for you out front."

"Who says I want to talk to you? There's not much more to say."

"Please, just come with me and talk," Leon pleaded. "I won't bother you again after this if you want me to leave you alone, but please come talk to me."

Brian sighed. "Fine, I'll talk to you. But make it quick and drop me off at home."

He hung up the phone and walked to Leon's car, a gold 1998 Pontiac Sunfire. He got in on the passenger's side and glared over at who he'd thought was his boyfriend until the night before. Leon was about an inch shorter than him and a shade or two darker in skin tone. His eyes were a dark brown and currently showed something resembling fear. Brian's gaze couldn't help but go to his lips, the most prominent feature on Leon's face. They were full and soft, just a bit lighter than his normal skin complexion. Brian bit his own lip, resisting the urge to kiss him. He would never do that again, not after this pain.

"You wanted to talk, so talk," he said irritably.

Leon started the car and drove off. "Look, I know I hurt you and I'm sorry. It was never my intention to hurt you."

Brian laughed bitterly. "You know, I always feared having this conversation with you, but I always thought I'd be the one saying that."

Leon gave a confused look. "Why?"

"You're older, but you were also the virgin. I'm not. I figured I'd get weak at some point. Shows what I know."

Leon looked uncomfortable. "So you've really only been with me this whole time?"

Brian glared at him. "Yes, jackass. I've only had eyes for you. I was more than willing to hold off for you. I wanted you. I still want you and it pisses me off."

"Why do you want me so much?" Leon asked.

Brian rolled his eyes. "You can't seriously be asking me this."

"I honestly want to know. Why am I so important to you?"

"The fact that you even asked me that just makes this so much worse. I have done nothing but show you that I care. So what I want to know is why I'm not nearly so important to you. This situation just tells me that I really meant nothing to you. You're just playing with me."

"No I'm not. I really didn't mean to do this to you. It's just that you're so young..."

"I'm barely two years younger than you," Brian cut him off.

"Yeah, but you're still in high school. You're not free during the day when I need you."

"Need me for what?" Brian demanded. "Prior to this Matt person, you hadn't had sex and didn't show any intentions to have sex. You don't need me for that. And how fucking hard is it to occupy yourself for eight hours a day? I'm in school from seven in the morning until two in the afternoon. And that hasn't even been a problem because I'm on summer vacation. How does that even factor into what you've done?"

"I know you're on vacation now but you're about to go back to school. And it's not like I work during the day. So we'll hardly ever see each other. We'll barely have time to talk."

"And this led you to fuck someone else *how*, exactly?" Brian asked bitterly.

"It just happened."

"Bullshit!" Brian shot back. "You planned it. You've been seeing him for months. You admitted it last night. Don't try to change the story now. You wanted him. And you really don't want me."

"That's not it at all." Leon scowled. "This is so hard to explain and I know this isn't going to come out right, but you're not what I'm really attracted to."

Brian sucked in a breath. That admission hit him as hard as any punch to the gut he'd ever taken. He couldn't speak. What could he say to someone he'd been seeing for months that made such a claim?

"Don't get me wrong. You're a great person. You're sweet and attentive and the most loyal person I've ever met. But I'm physically attracted to a different kind of guy."

Every word he said just drove a dagger deeper into Brian's heart. And yet Leon continued on.

"I like you a lot. I care for you. But I can't be more than a friend to you. I just don't feel the attraction. I was hoping that you could remain friends with me after this."

"You want me to be your friend?" Brian asked quietly.

"Yeah, I do," Leon answered. "Like I said, I care for you a lot. I like hanging out with you. I don't want you to walk out of my life. I just can't be what you want me to be."

"And it took you all of this time to tell me that. You couldn't have told me when I first came after you. You waited all these months until I actually fell for you to decide that I'm not attractive enough for you." Brian smirked humorlessly.

"It's not that you're not attractive. You're just not what I go for."

Brian finally looked at him. "That doesn't make any fucking sense. We've been together for months. Now you're not physically attracted to me. There's a lie in this somewhere and I can't see where it is. Yet you want me to be your friend. How do I even begin to act like your friend now? You want me to sit and listen to you talk about the other guys you're with now? How many are there? Is this Matt guy your boyfriend or just a random screw?"

Leon hissed. "I don't really know."

Brian almost laughed. "Oh, you don't know what he is? That makes this so much better. You let this guy fuck you and you're not even together. You and I actually were together and I never did more than kiss you. I waited for you, only for you to go screw this guy behind my back. But wait, it's not a random screw, is it? After all, you've been talking to him for a while. You planned it, right? You wanted him and to hell with my feelings. And then you called and told me about it. Why? Why didn't you just end it without ever telling me?"

Leon pulled up in front of Landon's apartment and parked, turning the car off. He sighed.

"I wasn't thinking. I was just so excited about things with him that I didn't think about you. I had to tell someone and I tell you everything."

Brian couldn't look at him any longer. "Everything? No, you don't tell me everything. If you did, I'd have known from the beginning that I'm ugly to you. I'm not your type. And I'd have never gotten into anything with you. You'd have just been that guy I spoke to in passing in the halls. Or maybe we would have been friends, but I would have known all along that that's all we'd be. There would be no attachment other than friendship here and we would just be hashing out all of the details. Instead, I'm sitting here barely able to breathe because this hurts so bad."

"I'm sorry." Leon reached for him.

Brian slapped his hand away. "Don't touch me. I don't want to be your friend. I wish I'd never known what you did. I wish you had just said it wasn't working and walked away. But instead you want me to stick around and torture myself. I can't do that. I can't stay around you when it hurts this much."

As he opened the door, Leon noticed the glint of a tear falling. He opened the door and got out to go after him, but stopped when he saw Landon pull up alongside him. Landon got out and gave a sharp look to Leon before focusing on Brian. He went forward and wrapped an arm around Brian, then turned and looked back at Leon.

"I'm fairly certain you've done enough, and I'm also fairly certain I've shot people for less. Get the hell out of here." Landon turned and led Brian inside, holding in the rage that his little brother was crying once again over the same jackass.

Chapter Fifteen

Landon decided against leaving home that night. Brian didn't really need to be alone. Strangely, Brian didn't fight him on it. Instead, he curled up under Landon on the couch and the two watched movies, until Brian fell asleep. Landon was dozing off as well, content with holding his younger friend when his phone went off. He silenced it to prevent from waking Brian and gently slipped away. He went into his bedroom and noticed that the number wasn't saved in his phone. That wasn't good.

"Hello?"

"We've got a problem." The voice was that of a man he really hoped he'd never hear from.

"What do you mean we've got a problem?" Landon demanded.

"It's Josh. He's gone off the deep end. He's been getting progressively worse. We can't control him and we don't know where he is now."

Landon scowled even though the speaker couldn't see him. "Damn it, Chris, I really don't want to deal with your problem. We agreed that you'd keep an eye on him and keep him the hell away from me and from here. I put up with him once a year when we visit the grave site, that's it."

"Look, I wouldn't have called you but he's probably headed your way. He's a lot worse now than he was when she died."

Landon couldn't hide his exasperation. "She didn't just die. She was killed. It's a whole lot easier to bear the load of guilt when you can admit that she was killed and we're all at fault. Now what the hell happened before he took off?"

"He's been pretty out of it lately. I'm pretty sure he's using something. I can't tell you what, but he's completely lost it. And he was ranting about you. He blames you."

Landon snorted. "That's nothing new. Funny how I get blamed when he's the ass that pulled a gun and fired it. What a fucking idiot. Any idea where he is?"

"If I knew, we wouldn't be having this conversation. I'd have come out there and dragged his ass back here. Listen, this may be the last time for him. I just have this weird feeling."

"If he's coming after me looking for a fight, you're damn right it'll be his last time. You'd better hope he steers clear of me. I'm not in any mood to deal with him. I've got enough problems in my life without dealing with him."

"I know, I know. Can you at least try to talk him down?" Chris pleaded.

"Since when did Josh ever listen to me?" Landon snapped. "If he'd listened to me eight years ago we wouldn't be in this mess and Shell would still be alive. I'm going out to look for him and if I find him we'll see how reasonable he is. If he presses the issue, then I hope you've made some form of peace with his death in your mind."

Chris sighed. "I'm surprised he lasted this long. All I'm asking is that you try."

"You know, if I never hear from you again, it'll be too soon." Landon hung up before he could reply, then dialed Kevin's number.

"What's up?" Kevin asked.

"I need you to sit with Brian for a while. I'm pretty sure he'll wake up and I don't want him here alone."

"What are you going to do?" Kevin questioned.

"Something I can't tell you about and no, I'm not about to sleep with someone else," Landon told him. "Please don't ask anything more about it. It's just an issue from my past that I really have to go handle."

Kevin sighed. "I'll sit with him but babe you really can't expect me to let this drop."

Landon rolled his eyes as far back as they'd go. "Honestly, you can blow me, and I mean that in the most insulting way possible. Now hurry up and get over here." He hung up and went back to check on Brian.

Brian was awake now and channel surfing. Landon sat next to him and wrapped an arm around him.

"I didn't mean to wake you," he told him.

"It's fine," Brian replied. "I woke up when I noticed you were gone. You're awfully warm so it got colder without you laying here."

Landon smirked. "Yeah, well I have to go out for a bit. Kevin's coming over to sit with you while I'm gone."

"That's cool I guess. But where are you going?"

Landon narrowed his eyes. "I'm sure you heard me on the phone with Kevin at the very least. I'm not telling you."

"Oh come on, you normally tell me everything," Brian argued.

"Not this time. There are a few things that I can't involve you in, kid. This is one of them."

Brian sighed. "Ok, but don't be out too long."

Landon laughed. "Yes, Dad."

Brian smiled slightly. "Shut up. I just don't like being alone and Kevin's not exactly a guy I can go lay up under."

At that, there was a knock on the door. Landon got up and let Kevin in, who kissed him quickly on the lips as he came in. Landon could only grunt in response. He couldn't say that he didn't like it. His defenses were weak when it came to Kevin.

Kevin grinned at him before taking a seat on the couch. Landon grabbed his keys and headed for the door.

"I should be back in a couple of hours. Don't text me or call me unless it's an emergency." He walked out of the door and closed it behind him.

"Do you have as bad of a feeling about this as I do?" Kevin asked Brian.

"Yep," Brian answered. "I've never come across anything that he won't tell either of us."

"I guess we just have to trust him." Kevin's face hardened.

Brian snorted. "I trust that he's into something big and probably illegal otherwise he'd have told us."

"Why do you say that?" Kevin asked.

"Because Landon is the guy we all call to handle someone that's giving us problems. He instills fear into our boyfriends and frankly Leon is lucky I was still outside earlier today or there would be blood stains on the sidewalk. He's never afraid to get his hands dirty. It's got to be something bigger than those type of things if he won't tell us anything." Brian thought for a moment. "I wonder if Renee knows anything."

Kevin raised an eyebrow. "You're going to call and ask, aren't you?"

Brian pulled out his phone. "Yep, because she has to know."

Kevin shook his head. "I'm probably never going to get laid again after this."

"That's totally not my problem." Brian found Renee's number and dialed.

Kevin knew Landon would be pissed if he found out about this but he was honestly worried. Landon always told either him or Brian everything. But if he didn't tell them, Renee was his best friend. Maybe she would put their minds at ease.

Chapter Sixteen

Landon knew Josh well enough to figure out where to start. This was already pissing him off to no end. He knew that there was no way in hell this would turn out good. He really didn't need old demons to creep up now. And this was not going to be easy. Josh wasn't going to be in a nice part of town. No, he was on the south side of town, and not the fun part. He knew where to go, but there was no way in hell that he was calling ahead. Matter of fact, he wasn't even going to park his car in front of the house he was going to. These people didn't need to know his phone number or what he drove. He parked a block over and walked around to the house he was going to. He needed to be in and out of this place as quickly as possible, so he only took a pocket knife with him.

Figures there's a party going on, he thought.

"You really should use your powers more."

Landon stopped with a sigh and turned to face the king. "It is seriously annoying how you follow me around. Go sit with your son for once."

"My son has me when he needs me. You need me more at the moment." Damien glared at him. "You are dealing with someone addicted to drugs. It's time you act like the Magus warrior you are. You have more than enough mental control over the power I've released. Stop acting so overly human."

"I've never been accused of acting human. I'm a calculating, moody, controlling bastard and you know it. But if

I'm allowed to really let loose with my power, I'll be more than happy to use it."

Damien sighed. "I should have known it would come to this. Fine, you are free to use your power however you wish from this point forward. You have my word."

Landon smirked. "Then step back and watch me work."

He continued on and stopped briefly as he spotted Josh's car, a 1996 Ford Taurus. This wasn't going to make his job any easier. He really needed help for this. If it had been earlier he'd have taken a bus here. But there wasn't much he could do now. He turned and continued up to the door. There was music blaring loudly and the house was full. It didn't matter to him. He was only here to collect the dumbass and get out. He ventured in and no one took special notice of him yet. That was good. Maybe he'd find Josh and get the hell out before the owner of the house saw him.

He looked around on the first floor but he saw no sign of Josh. But there was still the basement and the upstairs area. He'd rather avoid the upstairs area if at all possible. Frankly, the basement wasn't much better but it was likely that was where Josh was. So he headed down. There wasn't much lighting, only a few overhead lights hanging here and there. Fortunately for him, Josh was there under the one light that was actually on. Surprisingly, he was only playing cards. Landon stayed back and studied him.

Josh was short and stocky, with dark chocolate skin and eyes almost as dark. Currently, those eyes were a bit red and bloodshot. He was high as a kite. From here, he could tell that Josh had actually lost weight since the last time he'd seen him. His clothes were a bit loose on him. He already knew the guy's pants were sagging. He curled his lip in disgust as he looked at him. At the moment, he was hidden in the shadows, which worked for him. Extending his power out, he deepened the darkness surrounding him, ensuring that he was hidden from view until he wanted to be seen. He stepped away from the stairs as the small group at the table got up. The game was over. Landon inched closer to the table where Josh still sat, gathering up his winnings. Once everyone was upstairs, he stuck to the shadows and pulled the chair out across from Josh. Josh's eyes shot up as he tried to see who was across from him.

"Who's there?" he demanded.

"Your fucking keeper, apparently." Landon slammed his left hand on the table, startling him, and then shot his right hand forward to grab him by the throat, pulling him halfway across the table and finally leaning into the light so that he could be seen. His eyes were the brilliant ocean blue again, his power flaring outward to the point that even the very human Josh could feel it. "What in the fucking hell are you doing here and why shouldn't I bash your skull in now?"

"I'm not scared of you." Josh scowled at him. "And I go wherever I damn well please."

Landon tightened his grip, smirking as the other male coughed in an attempt to get air into his lungs. "Wrong answer, jackass. Remember who the hell you're dealing with. We had an agreement. You don't fucking cross the river. You stay in Illinois or anywhere else but St. Louis. You're high and probably drunk and I seriously regret making that damn promise to Shell. Now get your shit, grab your keys, and let's fucking go before I develop temporary amnesia."

Landon shoved him away and he coughed several times. He stuffed money in his pockets and walked towards the stairs with Landon right behind him. Thankfully, they made it out without incident.

"Give me your keys," he ordered.

Josh grumbled but did as he was told. The two got into the car and Landon started it up. He drove off quickly.

"Why are you here, Josh?" he asked irritably.

"I told you why," Josh replied defiantly.

"No, you didn't, and I'm very close to losing my patience." Landon pulled over in front of darkened houses not too far from his own car. "You know the agreement. You don't come here and I don't come there."

Josh scowled. "Screw you. Why should I listen to you?"

"Maybe because if you don't I'll put you in the ground," Landon shot back.

"Go ahead and try it."

Landon rolled his eyes and got out of the car. He walked around and opened Josh's door, quickly yanking him out again by his throat and slamming him spine first against the car.

"Listen here, if you really want to go, then don't just talk shit. Do something."

Josh shoved him back. "I fucking hate you."

Landon recovered quickly. "The feeling is mutual. Now swing, bitch."

Josh straightened up and looked him over. Landon knew what he was doing. He was looking for an opening. Damned if he'd give him one.

"You know this is all your fault," he said finally.

"How the fuck is it my fault?" Landon asked.

"So now you're playing dumb?" Josh snorted. "None of that shit would have happened if not for you. You and your little games."

Landon rolled his eyes. "Seriously? You're going to blame Shell's death on me? Fuck you. You're the one that pulled a damn gun."

"You slept with my girl!" Josh fired back.

"And how was I supposed to know that?" Landon asked. "She was my first. I was her first. Whenever we saw each other we slept together. I didn't ask if she had a dude and I really didn't care. It's simple. Once mine, always mine."

That did it. Josh rushed him in a football-like tackle. Landon had expected him to get sloppy, and caught him with a hard uppercut to the jaw. He knocked the slightly shorter man flat on his back, where he held his jaw and whimpered slightly.

"Do we really have to go through this?" Landon asked, exasperation evident in his voice as he tried his best to suppress the power threatening to escape his control and incinerate the human.

"Fuck you." Josh pushed himself up slowly, still holding his jaw. "Do you have any idea what I've been through? Do you know what it's like knowing you're responsible for killing someone you love?"

"Not only do I know what it's like, asshole, I also know what it's like to have to cover it up." Landon glared at him. "Did you forget why you're not rotting in jail and I'm not shanking you on a fucking regular for laughs? I handled all of it. You just cried like a little bitch."

"And you didn't cry at all!" Josh shouted.

113

"Go to hell. I cried plenty, but someone had to get shit done. I wasn't going to jail because you had to pull a gun. Who the fuck does that, anyway? You jumped on me and got your ass kicked, so you pulled a gun. And your aim fucking sucks so you shot her."

"You threw a knife asshole! You're not innocent in this."

Landon snorted. "I never said I was. But it's not all my fault. You could have handled things a lot better. She got caught in the middle because you can't control your temper. Which is also why you just got knocked on your ass."

Josh growled and tackled him successfully this time. Landon hit the grass hard with Josh between his legs, but he knew what was coming next. Josh rose up enough to throw a punch and Landon caught his fist. Landon then pulled him down and shifted his hips to wrap his left leg around the back of Josh's neck and connected his ankle under the back of his own right knee to trap Josh's shoulder against his own carotid artery. He then pulled down on the back of Josh's head enough to easily slow down the human's blood flow to his brain, which could render him unconscious. This was a hold known as sankaku-jime, or in English: the triangle choke.

"Are you done yet, or would you prefer a nice nap on some stranger's lawn?" Landon asked.

Without being able to truly catch his breath, all Josh could do was tap his leg in a sign of surrender. Landon released him and rolled to a seated position.

"I'm really tired of this and the next time you rush me I swear to God I'm rearranging your face," he warned.

Josh rolled to a seated position and held his shoulder, not saying anything.

"Why now?" Landon asked him.

"Because I want an end to everything," Josh answered softly. "I want an end to the guilt and hopelessness that I wake up with every day. I'm tired. In the end, we both know I killed her."

Landon said nothing. He remembered all of the details of that fateful day.

"And you know the real reason I flipped out. No one else knows. I never told Chris anything more. He only knows what he saw from a distance."

"What do you want from me?" Landon asked. "I can't absolve you. I can't say I understand all of it. I mean, I know I banged your girl, and I know we had a thing at one point too. But you can't honestly think I knew the two of you were together. You never said you had a girl and she never told me who her dude was."

"Is that supposed to make this all better for you?"

"Nope, I still deal with the guilt every day. I just don't let it rule my life. I don't bury myself in booze and drugs. I moved on, just like she asked me to. I still have the dreams every now and then. I replay that entire incident in my mind. I vividly remember being covered in her blood and riding with her to the hospital. I remember she died before we got there, and I remember promising to look after you and cease fighting." Landon snorted. "We're failing miserably at the last part."

The two fell silent, each entering into their own thoughts.

"Someone else knows what happened," Josh finally told him.

Landon turned to face him. "What?"

DRAKO

"I don't know who it is, but I've been getting calls and letters threatening to expose me. If he exposes me, it exposes you too, right?"

"Yeah, and a whole lot of others that helped me cover this up." Landon sighed. "Do you recognize the voice when the guy calls you?"

Josh shook his head. "I've never met him before. But there was no one around when it happened. No one but us and our friends, right?"

"I didn't see anyone, but I was rather busy trying to stop the bleeding and get rid of weapons to set it up to look like the result of a drive by. I don't think anyone was around that could have seen what happened, but I can't say for sure. I didn't even know Chris was there." Landon sighed again. "Is that the real reason you're here?"

Josh nodded. "I figured I might as well enjoy myself a little before I get prison time. Maybe I should just come forward and confess."

"And how will you explain what happened to the gun and why none of the rest of us ratted you out?" Landon asked.

"I'll figure it out. There's no need for everyone to go down with me. I'm the one that did it."

"Yeah, well I had my part in it, no matter how you downplay it."

Josh sighed and turned to face him slowly. "Look, it's time for me to face the music. Just do me a favor before I do it. Can we go by her grave one last time?"

Landon scowled. "Now?"

"Yes, now. Why not now?"

"It's the middle of the fucking night. Who visits graves in the middle of the night?"

Josh scowled. "We're already out. Let's just go visit it."

Landon pinched the bridge of his nose, a headache brewing. "You can't drive yourself and I'm not leaving my car here. I'll drive but you better be sure that this is really what you want to do."

Josh's face hardened. "I'm sure. Let's just go."

Chapter Seventeen

"I've got a feeling I know what this is about, but I totally can't tell you," Renee told Brian.

Brian scowled at the phone, which was held out in front of him on speakerphone so Kevin could hear. "Seriously?"

"Landon would kill me. If you heard the name Josh, it's got something to do with his past and he doesn't like talking about it. I only know because I've been around so long and was around when the whole thing went down. I can't tell you. He has to do it."

"Shit!" Brian muttered.

"All I can tell you is that you're right in thinking it's not a good thing," she added.

"So, should we be worried enough to try to find him?" Kevin asked.

"That depends. Did he grab his lock box?" Renee asked.

"Lock box?" Kevin questioned.

"He keeps it in the trunk of his car," Brian explained. "And we didn't go outside with him so I have no clue. But it's always in the car."

"Then I wouldn't go after him. You don't want to get caught up in what he's doing."

"Well, this sucks. I have a bad feeling about this," Brian mumbled.

"I'm not happy about it either. I was hoping Josh would never come around again. He always brings trouble."

"Can you tell me who this guy is?" Kevin asked. "I mean, is he an ex-boyfriend?"

Renee snorted. "Hell no, he'd never have dated that guy. You don't need to be worried about him being attracted to this guy at all. Their history isn't pleasant. That's really all I can tell you."

Kevin frowned. "I guess we'll just have to wait for him to get home."

Landon and Josh stood over the grave of their fallen loved one. Landon was by and large uncomfortable. He hated cemeteries, especially at night. He'd never visit Shell's grave if not for Josh insisting on it. He had loved her like no other, but he didn't want to live his life around her. She was gone and there was no changing that. Besides, he wasn't human. He could sense and see the restless souls of the dead who lingered there.

"Why do you insist on coming here?" he finally asked. "It's morbid and depressing."

"I like to think that she hears me better when I talk to her here," Josh answered.

"Look, I'm all for the spiritual thing and belief in the hereafter, but seriously, it's a fucking cemetery. It's well after midnight and I feel like the ghouls from Michael Jackson's Thriller video are about to pop out at me and start dancing."

Josh smirked. "Get real and stop being such a pussy. Besides, that wouldn't be so bad."

Landon rolled his eyes. "I like Michael, but fuck those ghouls and fuck cemeteries. How long do we have to stay here?"

"Not long." Josh knelt beside the gravestone, brushing dirt away from it. "Sitting here, I almost feel like she's forgiven me. I know she hasn't and I won't forgive myself either."

Landon merely frowned down at him without responding. He waited for a few minutes, tuning out Josh's chattering to a dead woman who actually wasn't hovering with the restless spirits in the cemetery and looked around. Something just didn't feel right.

"Dude, let's get out of here."

Josh stood up. "Fine, let's go."

The two headed back to the car when a car rode towards them. It was black with tinted windows, though neither could really tell the make or model of it. It turned, and as it did, the window came down. Landon's reflexes were slower than usual, even though he saw the gun being stuck out the window. It fired repeatedly and he went to drop to the ground, slower than he should have. Josh jumped in front of him, and was hit. Landon was startled as Josh fell back, knocking him to the ground. The car sped off and Landon pushed himself up to a seated position, finding Josh in his lap. Blood was already pouring and he was coughing up blood too.

"Shit! Hold on!" Landon scrambled to pull out his phone and dial 911.

Josh coughed again. "Too late. You know it."

"Don't you dare die now! I promised to keep after you and I won't break that."

More blood came up and Landon's clothes were quickly covered with it. He made the call to 911 but he knew that the gurgling sound he heard meant that it was too late. He was bleeding out. And Landon had no idea who in the hell had shot him. He'd seen nothing but the car itself, not the person inside. The person had shot at him, originally, not Josh. Which meant this wasn't over yet.

Damien appeared beside him. "Move out of the way. This little human has use to me."

Landon did as he was told with a scowl. "What the hell does that mean?"

"There's a force here that needs to be drawn out, and unfortunately you have no real healing power. I'm going to stabilize him and you will take him to the hospital. He will not awaken until his body has recovered." A white light emanated from the king's hands. "You are to track down the person in that car and draw out the person behind his actions. He is human. The power behind him is not."

"If you know who it is then why can't we just kill them?" Landon demanded.

"I'm not completely sure. I simply have a theory and if proven right, you have full authority to slaughter the culprit. This game is turning deadly and your past deeds, which I helped you cover up, are endangering my son." Damien's eyes met Landon's. "I tire of your inability to handle these situations in your life. You need to reach down and find the warrior within you before you lose everyone you hold dear. And if my son gets caught in the crossfire, I will forget your value as a warrior."

"You act as if I don't care about him. I've been around him long enough to actually care and I'll handle this situation myself, since I'm allowed to do it my way." Landon watched as the king worked on Josh. Though he cared fairly little for the human, he didn't want him dead by someone else's hand.

Chapter Eighteen

L andon didn't get home until after daylight. His clothes had been taken to be processed as evidence and he'd endured a barrage of questions that he had no answer for. Sure, he could give them an answer as to why they were in the graveyard, but he couldn't answer who knew they were there or who would want them dead. And without a doubt, Josh should have been dead. One of the shots had hit a main artery and he bled out. Another had hit his lung. Doctors thought it was a miracle he'd survived. It was close enough to the truth. And now, he got home to find Kevin and Brian asleep on separate couches in the living room. Both woke up when he opened the door, finding him dressed in sweat pants and a sweatshirt that he definitely hadn't been wearing when he left.

"What the hell happened and where are your clothes?" Kevin asked.

"It's a really long fucking story and I'm too tired to tell it again." Landon collapsed on the couch next to Brian.

"Tough shit, because you're totally telling us," Brian told him. "You were gone all night and you come back wearing something way different than what you had on when you left."

Landon glared at him. "Look, there was a shooting and blood got all over my clothes. The cops took my clothes and gave me this."

"Yeah, we're going to need more than that." Brian folded his arms across his chest.

Landon sighed. "If you must know, Josh is the last boyfriend of my ex-girlfriend, Shell. I made a promise to her when she died that I'd watch over him and I have, normally from a distance. And last night someone shot him as we were leaving her grave. I don't know who did it, but they were aiming at me."

Kevin frowned. "You're not telling us everything."

"No, I'm not. I refuse to. I don't want either of you caught up in what I'm in." Landon's gaze went to Kevin. "I don't need you trying to play hero."

"Too fucking bad, I'm going to do what I want." Kevin scowled at him. "You're clearly in over your head. What the hell is up between you and this Josh guy that someone would want to kill you over it?"

Landon closed his eyes and leaned his head to rest on the back of the couch. He really didn't want to tell this, so he sat trying to think of a way out of it. But in order to do what he knew had to be done, he had to tell them the truth or at least part of it.

"Look, Josh and I got into a fight that resulted in the death of my ex. Some years back, I slept with her on my birthday. She had a boyfriend at the time, Josh, and he found out. He jumped on me, we fought, and I was clearly winning. He went for a gun and I went for my knife. She got caught in the middle. She made me promise to look after him and not to fight with him again. That last part was impossible, but I did the important part. And I kept him out of jail. Now he's in the hospital and I have no clue who did it, but he told me that someone had been calling him and sending letters about this situation."

"So, what are you going to do?" Brian asked.

Landon took a few seconds to reply, resolving himself to what he had to do. "I'm sending you home for now until I feel like it's safe. Then I'm going to try my damnedest to keep from becoming a suspect and to keep what really happened to Shell from coming out."

"But won't they find the letters?" Kevin asked.

"Nope, I already took care of that."

Kevin and Brian looked at each other.

"So what else are you going to do?" Brian asked.

"Nothing you'll ever know about," Landon responded. "Now go get your stuff. Your mother is expecting you and you shouldn't have any problems."

Kevin snorted. "Ok, that solves your problem with him, but I'm not going anywhere."

Landon looked at him. "That's what you think. Just go home Kevin. I'll be fine and this will blow over sooner or later."

Landon stood up and went into his room. Brian also got up to pack his things, which were kept in Landon's room.

"You're not going to disappear are you?" he asked.

Landon was standing in front of his dresser, looking in the mirror. "No, Brian, I'm not going anywhere. I just don't want you caught up in this, I told you that."

"I had to make sure. You tend to disappear a lot." Brian began packing his things.

"I would never leave you completely alone." Landon turned to look at him. "This is only a precaution. When it's over, you can come back if you want."

He left the room to find Kevin standing at the window in his living room. Landon walked over and stood next to him.

"I'm worried about you," Kevin told him. "You're holding something back. You must feel like you're in danger."

"No, I feel like those I love will be in danger if they stay around me," Landon replied.

"I'm not a kid, and I'm not going to run and hide while you deal with whatever this is."

Landon smirked. "I love that you're trying to defend me, but in case you forgot, I can handle myself. I knocked you on your ass."

Kevin glared at him. "I wasn't trying to shoot you either."

"Trust me, I know the difference. It's hard to have come from St. Louis and not know the difference."

Kevin stared at him for several seconds. "I'm going home for now but you know I'm not going to stay away from you. I love you too much to be separated like that."

Landon rolled his eyes. "Please don't get mushy."

Kevin growled low in his throat. "Be glad Brian's here or we'd have a real problem."

Landon smirked. "Yeah, right. I'm totally shaking."

Kevin huffed. "Whatever, just call me when you get back home. I mean it."

He leaned down and kissed him on the lips before heading out of the door. Landon watched him leave the room, conflict filling his heart. Kevin was human while he was a Magus warrior with far too much power at his disposal. How could anything good come from this situation?

Chapter Nineteen

Landon kept himself away from everyone for the next few weeks. Perhaps he was just being paranoid but it certainly seemed as if that bullet had been meant for him. He didn't stay out of contact. That would be cruel. But no one came to his apartment, and he didn't go to see them if he could help it. The last thing he wanted was for anyone else to get caught in the crossfire. It shouldn't have been a surprise when he came home one night to find Kevin waiting for him.

"Kevin, what are you doing here?" Landon asked.

"I'm tired of you keeping yourself away from me," Kevin replied. "It may work for everyone else, but not for me. It's not fair, Landon."

Landon sighed. "Just come inside."

They went into the apartment and Kevin pinned Landon against the door.

"What's with the sudden aggression?" Landon asked.

"I don't like being shut out," Kevin told him. "I don't care about your past. I don't care who you think is after you. You don't get to shut me out. I love you too much for that, and I thought you loved me."

Landon hadn't struggled against him at all and continued not to as he spoke. "I *do* love you, and that's why I don't want you caught in the mess I got myself into."

Kevin looked into his eyes for several seconds. "Then why are we in an open relationship?"

Landon closed his eyes. "You know the answer to that."

Kevin leaned forward and rested his forehead against Landon's. "It's not fair. I love you and you love me. Neither of us wants anyone else. I haven't been with anyone else. Since you shut yourself off I haven't done anything but work and come home. What can I do to get you back for myself?"

Landon sighed and closed his eyes. "You hurt me Kevin. How am I supposed to get past that?"

"You have to try to trust me. I have done everything I can to show you that I care. I gave you space when you wanted it. I agreed to an open relationship even though I knew I didn't want anyone else. I've been torturing myself with the thought of you with some other man or even a woman. So even though I'm sure you suggested this to give yourself some variety and you've probably taken advantage of it, I'm still here. I still want you. And even though it hurts, I'll stay even if you shut me down. No matter how long it takes I'm going to be here with you however I can."

Landon opened his eyes and lifted Kevin's face up to look him in the eye. "So if I only wanted us to have an open relationship you would stay with me? What if I told you I wanted to have a three way every now and then?"

Kevin took a deep breath. "I'd find a way to make that work."

"What if I said I wanted Johnny?"

"I'd have to take you to a doctor to have your head examined. I know you're screwing with me and this really isn't the time."

Landon chuckled. "Is it really that far fetched? You and he used to have three ways all the time."

"With chicks and you're a lot different to me. I'd rather not share you with anyone, but if I must, I draw the line at Johnny."

Landon laughed outright. "OK, I can't take that any further. I think I'd rather stab myself than sleep with Johnny. Now, can we get off the door? It's not really that comfortable and we should be sitting for serious conversations."

Kevin released him reluctantly. "I don't like the sound of that."

"Don't think so negatively. It's honestly not going to be a bad conversation. It's almost over really."

Kevin sat on the couch and Landon sat next to him.

"I think we've gone long enough, and I can try to work past this," Landon told him.

"So, no more open relationship?" Kevin asked.

Landon nodded. "Back to normal. I guess you've suffered enough."

Kevin raised an eyebrow. "Oh, so I'm the only one that suffered?"

Landon shrugged. "I'm the one who inflicted the punishment. Any suffering I did was totally worth it."

Kevin grinned. "We'll see about that."

He quickly shoved him down and climbed on top of him, positioning himself between Landon's legs. Landon laughed softly.

"I don't think this is really a punishment," he commented.

"We're just getting started," Kevin replied.

Landon laughed again. "So, what now?"

"You don't get to come until I say so." Kevin began to undo his belt and pants. "You're going to beg for it."

Landon snorted. "Good luck with making that happen."

Kevin removed his lover's pants and underwear, eventually leaving him with nothing on but his shirt. Leaning down, he took Landon into his mouth, bringing him to full attention quickly. Knowing his lover all too well, he slipped a hand under him, his middle finger playing at his entrance. He heard a low moan come from Landon and removed his mouth. Landon glared down at him and Kevin grinned.

"Relax. You know I'm not done." Kevin lowered his head, licking down Landon's shaft and balls until he reached the entrance. Landon tensed and Kevin rose up again, coming back up his shaft and taking him in wit mouth again. Leaving his hand under Landon, he forced him to buck his hips up and down, sliding in and out of his mouth. When Landon began to buck faster than Kevin intended, he removed his mouth again and Landon groaned in frustration.

"Are you ready to beg yet?"

Landon scowled. "You're good, but not that good."

Kevin laughed. "Big talk, little man."

He lifted Landon up off the couch and carried him into the bedroom. There was a lot of time to be made up for.

Chapter Twenty

D *ream/Memory:*
    The glitz and glamour of Avalon was still unsettling to Landon. His mother had taken him there several times over the years for these gatherings among the nobility. As the heir apparent to the lands of both of his parents, he was obligated to attend these gatherings even if he wasn't much of a diplomat. In fact, he was a warrior, as were his parents. But the Magi and their politics were endless and deadly. He had no choice in dealing with it.

Standing in the grand ballroom of the king's palace, he half listened to the inane prattle some nobles were spouting around them. His mother, Eliza Augusta, was no more interested than he was but she hid it well. The golden brown skinned matriarch may have appeared to be just another noble beauty, dressed as she was in a long purple gown with her magnificent sandy brown hair hanging freely, but those gathered knew better. Power radiated from her naturally and her bright sky-blue eyes seemed to see right through anyone they looked upon. She dressed this way on purpose, as Landon was actually wearing his armor. It wasn't heavy, just simple silver armor that allowed him to maneuver. Magi metal was different from that of the mortal world after all. There was a sword attached to each hip, the one on the right a short straight sword while the one on the left was full length. The hilts of both were simple: black with a solid gold pommel and a guard just big enough to keep his hand from sliding to the blade. He could draw either quickly, which was the point of their design. He was, for appearances' sake, his mother's knight and guardian.

"You appear to be as bored as I am."

Landon took a moment to brush his own long dark brown hair from his face before looking to the speaker beside him. The male in question was a bit taller than him and broader around the shoulders. He had the same brown skin tone as Landon, but his eyes were a golden honey brown instead of the blue Landon had inherited from his mother. He was stunning to see, even at the young age of eighteen years old, with a smile that would make even their own kind swoon.

"Damien," Landon nodded in greeting.

Damien grinned. "Just can't bow, can you?"

Landon rolled his eyes. "Only in your dreams. Shouldn't you be up on a pedestal looking down on everyone?"

Damien chuckled. "It's boring sitting up high. Besides, I may be a prince but I'm not the heir to the throne yet."

Landon grunted. "That's a formality and you know it."

Damien's expression became far less readable. "There are many forces at work here. Something has been amiss for a while."

Landon frowned. "You know something?"

Damien glanced around. "Not here. Do you think you can slip away?"

Eliza simply waved a hand to dismiss him so Landon stepped away with the prince.

"So, what's the situation?" he asked.

Damien wouldn't respond until they reached the gardens outside. The prince flicked his wrist and Landon felt his power spread out. It was a barrier to keep others away.

"How long have you been here?" he asked.

"It's difficult to tell, but maybe a couple of hours," Landon answered.

"Haven't you noticed the absence of the king?"

Landon paused. "I hadn't thought about it."

"Only a few know what today is really about. Have your parents met with any other nobles?"

Landon shrugged. "A few have requested audiences with my mother but I neither know nor care what my father does."

Damien sighed. "It would be handy if you would at least keep in contact with him. I have no idea how he might move."

"I still don't care until he's dead." Landon's expression hardened. "What's going on?"

"Today is about naming the next king," Damien admitted. "But, I'm not terribly popular among some of the nobles."

"I can't imagine why," Landon said sarcastically.

Damien playfully shoved him. "I'm serious. I'm going to have to fight for this but I'm not sure I can do so on my own."

Landon folded his arms across his chest and studied him for several moments before responding. "You need a champion."

Damien sighed. "Obviously. You know I haven't trained to be a warrior."

"I'm aware, but you're powerful in your own right," Landon assured him. "You can hold your own."

Damien raised an eyebrow, surprised at the reassurance. "Are you hesitating? Perhaps waiting to see which way the wind blows?"

Landon didn't feel any real hesitation for himself. Damien was certainly flamboyant and sometimes irritating, but in truth they got along well. They had grown up together, though Landon was three years older. His mother was highly respected in the court and by the king. However, siding with Damien against the other nobles required his mother's approval at least.

Damien was no fool and figured his line of thought. "You aren't sure if your mother would allow you to support me."

Landon felt no need to lie. "It's not like I knew this would be an issue. The politics are her arena. I do the fighting."

"Your mother has always been very warm to me and her opinion holds sway with the others." Damien stepped in closer to take his hands. "Besides that, you and I have known each other all my life. Your support means the most."

Landon sighed, already resigned to what he would have to do. "I will do what I can. How soon will I have to make this choice?"

Damien avoided his gaze, a sure sign of Landon not liking his answer.

"So it begins tonight then." Landon reached out to turn Damien's face to him. "No one will harm you while I'm here. I'll deal with the fallout later."

Damien breathed a sigh of relief. "Good. I'm sure there will be violence tonight and I don't like my chances alone."

"No one here will get within striking range of you," Landon promised. "Now, let's get back inside."

Chapter Twenty-One

It was 2 AM when Landon's phone went off, waking him from his stroll down dream memory lane. His phone never went off at that time, not when Kevin was lying next to him. Opening one eye, he looked at the brightly lit screen.

"What is it, Denise?" he asked as he picked up the phone.

"Come quick, Brian's in the hospital! It's..." she sobbed.

"Which hospital?" Landon was instantly alert.

"Christian Northeast."

"I'm on my way." He hung up and got out of bed, waking Kevin.

"What's wrong?" he asked groggily.

"I don't know, but Brian's in the hospital. You can stay here but I have to go."

Kevin shook his head and got up to get dressed too. "Someone has to go to restrain you if whatever happened wasn't an accident."

Landon didn't argue, just put on the closest clothing he could find and led the way out of the house. When they got to the hospital, Brian had been admitted and they were shown to his room despite the late hour. Denise was sitting next to the bed in a chair, her eyes bloodshot from crying. Brian was asleep, hooked up to an IV and a machine to watch his vitals. Landon looked over him to find any bruises but saw none. This wasn't the result of a fight.

"What happened?" he asked Denise, placing a comforting arm around her.

"I came into his room to check on him. It was late and his light was still on, so I thought I just needed to wake him up to get him into bed. But he wouldn't wake up and there was a bottle of pills next to him. The whole bottle was gone so I called an ambulance. He's been out the whole time."

"What happened since he came back home? I thought everything was ok."

"So did I. He didn't mention anything being wrong. I don't know what's happening with him."

"How long have you been here?"

Denise looked at her watch. "About four hours."

"Go home and get some sleep. I'll stay here with him tonight. I'll call you if he wakes up." Landon helped her up. "Kevin can drop you off."

"I'd really rather stay," Denise argued.

"You're tired and can barely keep your eyes open. Go home and sleep. He'll be fine." Landon looked at Kevin. "Do you mind?"

"I got it. I'll be back in a few." Kevin took Denise's arm and led her out.

Landon sighed and sat in the chair Denise had just vacated. He took Brian's limp hand in his own.

"Baby boy, what the hell happened? What went so wrong that you would do this to yourself?" Landon watched his face but saw no response. "We're going to talk when you wake up kid. And you're going to wake up."

Several hours later, Brian did indeed wake up. Landon had fallen asleep with his head on the edge of the bed. Kevin had gone to sleep in a chair at the foot of the bed, his head leaning against the wall. Brian gave himself a few minutes to adjust and figure out where he was before moving enough to wake Landon up. It didn't take Landon long to recover his senses.

"How long have you been awake?" he asked.

"Only a few minutes." Brian pushed himself to sit up.

"So, are we going to talk about this now or am I going to have to wait on a doctor to tell me what I want to know?" Landon helped him adjust the bed to sit up more comfortably. "Why, Brian? What the hell happened?"

Brian sighed. "I don't actually know. I didn't really plan on it. I don't know why the idea would ever occur to me. It just did."

"These things don't just pop into your head for no reason. What's been going on?" Landon took his hand. "Does this have anything to do with Paul or Leon?"

Brian closed his eyes. "Can we hold off on this for a while please?"

Landon stared at him for several seconds. "Alright, I'm going to go call your mom. You really scared her. We'll talk about this sooner or later, preferably sooner."

He left the room and pulled out his phone to make the call. The sight that greeted him pissed him off. Leon was actually making his way to the room.

"Oh, hell no." Landon strode forward quickly, not taking the time to think. Leon caught sight of him just before Landon caught hold of his arm and forced him to the elevators, pressing the down button.

"Ah, what the hell is your problem?" Leon demanded, snatching his arm out of Landon's grip.

"I'm the absolute *last* person you want to fuck with right now. You don't get to come in here and fuck with his head, not today. We're already in a hospital and if you don't want to be in the ICU, you'll get your ass in this elevator with me."

Leon scowled but stepped into the elevator. Landon followed him and took them down to ground level. When the doors opened again, he shoved Leon out ahead of him.

"Damn, I can walk out on my own," the younger man muttered.

"Shut the fuck up and move," Landon growled.

He followed the young man all the way to his car. Once there, he pushed him up against the car and held him there.

"Now what the blue fuck did you do to my boy this time?!" he demanded.

Leon glared back at him. "I didn't do anything. I'm trying to be his friend."

"I could have sworn he said he didn't want to be your friend. Why the fuck are you still bothering him?" Landon pulled him forward only to slam him against the car again. "It's like you're *trying* to make me fuck you up. You're not going to keep toying with my boy's emotions. He's not your fallback guy. You either get it together and get with him or leave him alone."

"You can't keep me away from him. I care about him, and his mom told me what happened. I didn't do anything to make him do it, but I came to check on him."

Landon scowled. "Don't fucking insult me. You have been playing him since day one. He may not be willing to do what's best for him but clearly something is wrong and you're part of the problem at least. If I end up here with him again, it'll be because *you're* the one in the hospital bed, if you catch my drift. Now get the fuck in your car and drive off. Don't call him, don't text him, and don't try to come up here when you think I'm gone. I'll be here until he leaves and if I catch you here, I might just decide to toss you out of a window next time. Now go."

He stepped back and watched Leon get into his car and drive off. He was trying his best not to resort to the darkest of his old ways, but he really wanted to stab that guy in the throat.

Chapter Twenty-Two

Landon went to Brian's house to clean out his room. He made sure to remove any and all prescription medications from the room and even over-the-counter pills were hidden in his mother's room. Paul was conspicuously absent, not that he cared much. It was easier when he wasn't around. As he finished up, Denise brought Brian home.

Brian entered his room and wasn't surprised at all to see Landon there. He walked in and sat at the edge of the bed, lowering his head with a sigh. There would be no more avoiding the conversation. Landon had been patient while he was in the hospital, but now it was time to come clean. He didn't even look up as Landon sat next to him, not until Landon forced him to.

"You know the question already," he said simply, looking into the younger man's eyes.

Brian wanted to look away, but Landon had his hand on his chin in a very clear message to keep eye contact. "Everything just felt overwhelming. I don't know why but it was suddenly just too much to handle. I've been going through a lot, and I guess it all just caught up to me."

"I know you've gone through a lot, but it's still kind of odd to just decide to take your own life. It's not like you." Landon removed his hand from his chin. "So, what changed?"

"The doctor said it may have something to do with some medication I was taking and had to stop taking suddenly."

Landon frowned. "What medication? Since when have you been on meds?"

"Since fifth grade, actually," Brian told him. "I never told you. I don't tell anyone. But I was put on anti-depressants and now I can't get them. Being without them so suddenly apparently made things worse for me. So, now we're here."

Landon closed his eyes and took a deep breath. "I can understand the effects of going without making things harder to deal with. But what were you feeling? Why didn't you call me?"

"I just felt...." Brian paused, searching for the words. ".... alone and unloved. All the fighting between Mom and Paul and you and Paul, then everything with Leon and problems at school was just too much. I just felt like it'd be easier to end it all."

Landon wrapped an arm around his shoulder and pulled him into an embrace. "Kid, you are *never* unloved. You have to know your mother loves you. Everyone makes crappy decisions sometimes but in the end she wants what's best for you. And I definitely love you, more than you know. And I know he's not around as much as you'd like, but your father loves you too. We all have rough times, but since I've been around you mine are a lot easier to handle."

Brian didn't respond, instead just leaning in closer and wrapping his arms around him.

"I don't want you to ever feel like you can't talk to me, even if I can't come to see you. I'm always here for you, no matter what situation I'm in. You're never alone, Brian, never. You have to remember that."

"You have enough going on without me running to you with every little problem," Brian said quietly.

"Whatever I have going on is not more important than you. Nothing with you is unimportant to me, Brian." Landon lifted his face to look him in the eyes. "No matter what kind of fucked up situation I find myself in, if you need me, you call me. I can always talk. If you need me here with you, say so and I will get here from wherever I am. This situation will never happen again while I'm around, do you hear me?"

Brian nodded and buried his face in Landon's chest. Landon couldn't help but hold him tighter. His young friend was hurting and realistically there wasn't anything he could do to help him other than what he was doing right at that moment.

KEVIN STOOD OUTSIDE of the door, watching in silence. This was Landon's moment with Brian, but like Landon, he cared for Brian too. Most of all, he loved Landon and anything that hurt Landon hurt him too. He frowned a bit as he realized that. He loved Landon like no one else. Matter of fact, he didn't think he'd ever been in love before Landon. It was a strange thought. He'd fallen for Landon so easily that he hadn't realized he'd never been in love before him.

He backed away and stepped outside of the house as the realization hit him. He sat outside on the stairs and waited patiently, looking off absently over the neighborhood. Several minutes later, the door opened behind him and Landon sat down beside him.

"What's on your mind?" Landon asked.

"Nothing much. I just left out to give you two time alone," Kevin answered.

Landon gave him a bland stare. "I know you better than that."

Kevin smiled. "It's nothing really. It's kind of goofy and sappy. You don't do sappy."

Landon laughed softly. "Normally, you'd be right, but you don't do sappy either. I want to hear it."

Kevin stayed silent for a few seconds before responding. "I just realized that I've never really loved anyone before you. I was watching you with Brian and I realized how much I really hate to see you unhappy. And it hurts that I was the cause of you being unhappy recently."

"That actually wasn't that sappy. It's just how you feel."

Kevin rolled his eyes. "It's sappy and you know it. It doesn't really begin to cover how I feel about you either."

Landon chuckled. "But it's cute coming from you because it's so unexpected. I can deal with a little bit of sappiness every now and then."

Kevin wrapped an arm around him. "Well you got it. I love you, Landon."

Landon leaned in to rest his head on Kevin's shoulder. "I love you too, Kevin. Thanks for helping out with all this."

"You didn't need to do it all alone. Your loved ones are my loved ones now, especially Brian. This wasn't a chore for me. I want to do anything for you that helps make things easier."

Landon closed his eyes and exhaled. "Being around you is always a help to me."

Kevin laughed softly. "Not always. We're coming out of a real rough patch."

"No relationship is perfect, Kevin, but we're together. That's something for now."

The two look down the street and noticed a car driving far too slowly in their direction. Landon straightened up, noting the tinted windows of the car. It looked far too familiar.

"Fuck!" Landon swore, rising quickly and pulling Kevin with him. "Get in the house, now!"

Kevin's eyes widened but he moved quickly. As he went inside, Landon saw the window roll down. He dashed into the house, closing the door behind him.

"Everyone get to the back of the house and get down now!" Landon ordered.

Thankfully, everyone in the house paid attention, as gunfire sounded rapidly. Windows shattered and Denise screamed. Everyone hit the floor out of instinct as bullets peppered everything in the house. Landon slid along the ground to the back door and went out of the house. Reaching for a weapon, all he had was a knife, his favorite weapon, but not much good against whatever the hell was shooting up his friend's house. It was all he had to work with and damn it he would not lose anyone he loved here today. He dashed around to the front of the house as the car ceased firing and sped off. At least he saw it clearly, and most importantly, the license plates. That car looked awfully familiar, and not just from the night Josh was killed. He wasn't sure where else he'd seen it but he'd make sure he found out.

He went back into the house and found Kevin sitting up against the wall, blood pouring from his shoulder. As he rushed to his lover's side, he could hear Denise on the phone, making the 911 call. Kevin had one hand on his shoulder and was getting pale. He was still lucid as Landon leaned next to him.

"Where'd you go?" he asked, pain evident in his voice.

"Don't worry about it, Kevin," Landon replied, examining the wound. "Are you hit anywhere else?"

Kevin grunted in pain. "No, just my shoulder. I didn't go down fast enough."

Brian ran in with towels, which Landon held to the wound.

"Is he going to be alright?" Brian asked.

"The bullet passed through. When the paramedics get here he'll be fine," Landon answered roughly.

"How can you tell?" Kevin asked.

"There's a lot that you don't know about me, Kevin." Landon looked into his eyes. "Now shut up and stop moving."

Within a few minutes, they heard the sirens. It was time to talk with the police again, something Landon would rather have avoided.

Chapter Twenty Three

F*lashback*
Landon had returned to his mother's side after speaking with Damien. Eliza was an observant woman and had excused the people around her before he returned.

"Tell me you have news."

Landon gave the slightest of smiles at his mother's directness. "There is an issue with the throne. We'll have to put our support behind someone tonight."

Eliza didn't seem surprised. "You want to support Damien."

Landon gave no response because it wasn't a question. The real question is what his mother would decide.

"He is not a warrior yet so he will need a champion," she continued. "I imagine he has asked for your assistance. What did you tell him?"

"Only that no harm would come to him tonight," Landon answered honestly. "Beyond that, the decision isn't exactly mine."

Eliza rolled her eyes. "You are the heir to my estate and station. It's time for you to make some decisions. If you wish to support him, then we shall."

"Is there any reason that I shouldn't?" Landon questioned.

"Not particularly, no," Eliza answered. "There was always the option of remaining neutral. But Damien is wise enough to see a powerful ally, and truth be told, your power will only increase. Better to have you at his side than possibly rising against him."

"I don't even like being heir to you and the asshole you made me with. I definitely wouldn't go for the throne. He's better suited to it."

Eliza shrugged. "You're not wrong. Speaking of said asshole, where is he?"

"Not here," Landon bit out. "I was expecting him or the bitch to be here."

Eliza grunted but said nothing more. It seemed their attention was being demanded. There was a gathering around the throne, so it seemed the moment had arrived.

"Nobles of Avalon, we have gathered you here to deliver the somber news that our king, Arturo Adaire, has departed this life and as such a new king must be crowned. His heir apparent is his son, Damien Adaire. You are here to acknowledge and swear fealty to the new king."

"Preposterous!" came the first objection.

"He is still a child!"

Eliza sighed as the objections came from several directions. To be honest, they got redundant quickly. She flicked her wrist in the direction of the throne as a clear sign to Landon. In a flash, he stood next to Damien, who barely concealed his surprise. The objectors fell silent.

"At which point did it become proper to whine, bitch, and complain solely because your sovereign is younger than you?" Landon asked. "Arturo has but one living child. On what grounds other than his age and supposed inexperience do you object to his succession of the throne?"

"You are but three years older than he is, another child!"

Landon's eyes came to rest on this particular objector. "Dwayne, your objections are most predictable. But you do realize I am heir to two of the most powerful nobles among you, right?"

"Then let the heads of the house speak instead!"

The Magus in question soon found himself unable to move as a flare of power filled the room. His dull black eyes widened and if he had been able, his small, lithe frame would have been shaking. The crowd parted as Eliza slowly walked forward.

"My dear Lord Dwayne Aubrey, did you think that my son would not have my full support in anything that he does?" Eliza moved with the knowledge that all eyes were on her. "He is the heir to my house and that of his father. His decision to support the throne stands for both houses, and I would suggest you follow suit."

Landon extended a hand to help his mother ascend the dais to stand beside him. It wasn't inherently necessary. It was a show for the other nobles, a sign of her support and passing of authority to him, at least in this instance. She then gestured to Damien that he should take his seat on the throne. This emboldened the younger Magus, as he sat with the full confidence that the throne belonged to him.

"This matter is very simple to resolve," he told the crowd. "You may accept this and swear fealty, at which point you are allowed to continue your rule. Or you may challenge me for the throne, but do be warned, I am a lot smarter than I look. If you insist on challenging me, you will face my champion."

Landon caught the slightest of movements in the crowd of nobles. He reached over and caught a dagger hurled at the king's head, while Damien, to his credit merely sat with his head on his hands and a bemused smile on his face.

"I daresay that someone thinks they can challenge you." Damien hid no amusement from his voice. "Please show them the error of their ways."

Landon twirled the dagger between his fingers. "I'm going to make this simple for some of you. You are the biggest bunch of arrogant simpletons I've ever had the displeasure of being in a shared space with. Your minds are open books. Did no one teach you to shield your thoughts? As such, I know exactly who in this room is supporting the new king, and who thinks they can take his place. You have approximately ten seconds to run before I put you all down. Those loyal, by all means, remain to swear your fealty."

Damien's amused expression didn't leave his face even as he watched some of the nobility begin to shuffle. They didn't make their decisions quickly enough as suddenly the room was filled with a burst of power that blew the entire crowd backwards. Landon extended his hand and several people burst into flames. In moments, their bodies were reduced to ashes. The others seemed to be spurred into action finally. Landon chose not to draw his swords at all, deeming that a show of power would be more effective. From his left, he saw a noble launch himself through the air. Landon flicked his wrist and incinerated him as well.

Panic began to set in as they realized the nightmare before them. Landon radiated power as he stepped down off the dais and walked through the ballroom, incinerating specific targets as he did. The room lit up in the bright orange glow of flames that slowly seemed to engulf most of the ballroom.

"Is it just me, or does no one understand how powerful he actually is?" Damien asked Eliza.

"Not many understand how much he restrains himself," Eliza agreed. "To be fair, this is rather restrained."

"Good thing we've always been friends," Damien muttered.

A wall of fire had hidden most of the room from view, interestingly not damaging anything other than the people Landon targeted. Moments later, he stepped through the fire untouched and strode confidently back to the dais. The flames vanished as quickly as they'd sprung up, revealing a severely depleted crowd.

"That was a bit more than I expected," Damien commented.

"Then be specific in the future," Landon replied.

Damien conceded that point. "No matter, it was a strong showing from my champion. Care to finish up?"

Landon turned to the remaining nobles. "Just so you know, I am not the most tolerant champion. You were spared solely because I sensed no willingness to challenge the king. Now, he's sitting on the throne and those loyal to the throne must swear fealty."

Those remaining gathered closer again and one by one, took a knee and bowed their heads in front of the throne. The attendants by the throne followed suit, with Eliza and Landon joining in last after they were certain no one else intended to strike out. Damien raised his head finally.

"With this, you are now bound to my service on the throne. Those who perished here today will have their lands divided among you. For now, you will return to your homes until such time as I call for you to gather again. Spread word that any act against me is treason and will be met with the force you saw here today. Now rise."

Everyone stood together and dispersed quickly, leaving Landon and Eliza alone with the new king and his attendants.

"Thank you, Lady Eliza," Damien said earnestly.

Eliza raised an eyebrow. "Landon did all the work."

"Yes, but if you had not given him leave to stand with me, I fear tonight would have gone far differently," Damien replied.

"There was no reason for me to go against you," Eliza told him. "You are the rightful king. See that you rule with dignity so that I never change my mind." She looked to Landon. "I will see myself home. Settle in here and be in touch soon."

Landon nodded his acknowledgment before she vanished. Damien waved a hand to dismiss the attendants and breathed a sigh of relief.

"I honestly thought this would end up worse," he commented.

"You know it's not done," Landon pointed out. "More than just those here will have an issue or see a reason to make a play to take the throne from you. Not all of the nobles of Avalon were here."

"Then I suppose I'll have to learn to put all this power to use in actual battle." Damien sighed. "I'll need your help."

"It's what I'm here for," Landon assured him. "You'll catch on quick enough. You have the talent. It's just the will that's lacking."

"You're never going to be a deferential servant are you?"

Landon smirked. "Hell no. Someone has to keep you grounded. Now let's get out of here. Someone needs to clean up all the ashes and air out that burnt smell."

Chapter Twenty-Four

Landon came out of his thoughts and memories to finally get things done. Hours later, Kevin was in a hospital room and Landon had put Denise and Brian up in a hotel room. He didn't give a damn about Paul, though he was fairly certain he'd end up in the room too. Before he left them, he had a word with Brian outside.

"Look, I know what this is about, and I don't want you caught in the crossfire any more than you already are. I'm still here for you. If you really need me, call and I'll be here. But I need to settle this before I lose anyone else." Landon took the young man's face in his hands. "I'm not abandoning you. You're not alone. My phone will stay on. I just won't be around unless it's an emergency."

Brian nodded. "I get it. But please be careful. You don't want to lose us, and I don't want to lose you."

Landon hugged him. "Be careful kid. Avoid any black cars with tinted windows and don't go near my house. I'll be in touch when I can."

Kevin was not nearly so understanding.

"You are *not* leaving me in a hospital to go running after some random person with the audacity to fire on us in broad fucking daylight!"

Landon sighed. "Kevin, you're not in any condition to stop me. Besides, I know this is someone connected to my past and there's too much at stake for me to just let it slide."

"Then let the police handle it! Why the fuck are you trying to do it alone?!"

"Because if the cops are involved and actually manage to find this person, I'm pretty damn sure I'm going to prison!" Landon hissed.

"Then at least wait until I'm out of here," Kevin pleaded.

"Kevin, your arm is in a sling and you're out of your element here. I love you, but I don't need you involved in any of this. I don't need you to know anything that puts you any more at risk. I need you here and safe."

Kevin scowled at him. "I need you here with me and safe. Not running after whoever this is."

Landon frowned back at him. "You're being petty. You know I'm right. If I don't do anything then this person will keep coming after me and if the police manage to catch him, then all of my secrets start coming out."

"How many secrets *do* you have?!" Kevin demanded. "How much could anyone possibly have on you to make you so damn scared?!"

"I'm not scared!" Landon fired back. "But I know the type of people I've dealt with. Whoever this is wants to hurt me. They want to hurt me by killing anyone close to me. I don't need to lose anyone else I love like this."

"I'm not going to just sit back and let you go."

"I don't give a damn if you sit, stand, lay down, jump up, or anything else, but you know I'm going."

Kevin tried to sit up, but Landon placed a hand on his chest.

"Stop. You're not ready to be released yet and you know I'm going to go find this guy. Don't make this any harder than it has to be."

Kevin lay back and looked up into Landon's eyes. "Landon, I don't want you putting yourself in danger. I don't want...."

Landon kissed him to stop the next words. He knew what they would be and he didn't want Kevin to speak them aloud. They didn't need to be said. The kiss was needy, deep, and desperate. Kevin felt like it was a goodbye and clung to his lover, taking control of the kiss like a man possessed. Eventually, Landon pulled away.

"Kevin, I love you, and I don't think I'll be gone long. Just let me know when you leave and don't go to my house under any circumstances." Landon rose and left quickly. He would have to use less conventional means to track whoever was after him. Good thing he wasn't human after all.

Landon had reached his car when he realized something felt off to him. It was too quiet, and the parking lot of the hospital was completely devoid of anyone. He stepped back away from his car, his senses on high alert. This wasn't a natural quiet.

He caught a glint out of the corner of his eye and that was all he needed to know this was an attempt at a trap. Unfortunately for his fellow Magi, they weren't nearly strong or fast enough to catch him unaware. He reached up and effortlessly caught a blade between his first two fingers and thumb.

"Wow, whoever sent you was a real idiot. Or they wanted you to die." Landon flicked his wrist and snapped the blade of the sword, much to the surprise of the man attacking him. He caught the broken blade and stabbed him in the side of the neck with it, letting him fall to the ground.

Just as quickly as he dispatched this one, another was at him. There was no time to study the features of this group, but he knew they were his kind, not humans. Another sword came at his head and he fell backwards into a flip, kicking the blade in their hand up into the air. Once he was on his feet again, he caught the blade and stabbed this attacker in the chest. By his count, there were roughly eight others and all of them were surrounding him. Fortunately for him, his old instincts had kicked into overdrive. Using the blade he'd taken, he went on the attack, taking only moments to cut down all of them.

"This seems like a waste of life." Damien appeared leaning against his car. "Surely they had to know that this wasn't enough to stop you, even if you're not at full strength."

"If I had to guess, no one but my mother would be able to tell that I'm not at full strength," Landon replied. "Then again, I don't know how many people you told why I'm stuck here anyway."

Damien gave him a dull stare. "The king doesn't share unnecessary information with the servants. Didn't you teach me that?"

Landon shrugged. "Probably. I'm not fully back so my memories come in flashes. Now, do you have any objection to me hunting down the human involved in this?"

"Already know who it is, do you?"

Landon asked. "Yeah, I know who it is. Just didn't think he'd matter in the grand scheme of things. Now, can I handle it however I want or do you have some arbitrary rules to add on?"

"If this person shot your boyfriend and put my son's life in danger, I'd rather you ensure he can never do so again," Damien answered. "Do as you wish but be quick about it."

Chapter Twenty-Five

Landon found the car exactly where he thought he would, the barbershop where he'd met Xavier. He parked across the street, not really believing his luck. What kind of idiot did a drive by in their own car and kept the car in town in plain sight? Landon didn't even bother to step out of the car. He was seething with anger. This stupid little human had the audacity to not only come after him, but to attempt to hurt those he loved. The little bastard was just lucky Landon didn't want to draw too much attention to himself.

"So, what are you going to do?" Damien was once again sitting in the backseat of his car.

"I'm going to send a little message my way." Landon glanced back at him. "I have your word that I'm free to act as I desire in this situation, right?"

The king nodded. "You have my word as the king of Avalon that you are free to act in whatever way you deem necessary."

"Excellent." Landon's power surged free, shedding the glamour he'd been born with into this life to once again reveal his true beauty. Sky blue eyes were practically glowing as he looked at the car and willed the power he'd been so hesitant to use before. As he sent forth the power that caused the car to explode, literally, in a bright orange ball of flames, images flashed through his mind. He saw what appeared to be himself on a battlefield, covered in blood and surrounded by a strange bright blue aura that continuously flared outward.

"Landon!" The king slapped him, forcing him to return to himself.

"What the hell was that?" Landon asked.

"With the release of your power will come the release of your memories of your past life. So far you only remember trauma from the earlier part of that life. You will slowly but surely remember all."

Landon glared at him. "You could have told me that sooner."

"I need you to be that warrior again, but not just the heartless killing machine that secures my throne. That was the point of your reincarnation into this life."

"You really need to be a bit clearer on what exactly I did one of these days to end up this way. But for now, I'm going to finish off this situation. Go away or whoever you're looking for won't reveal themselves."

As the king vanished, Landon continued to his destination, Xavier's apartment. He examined the building to determine how best to get inside. There was a front and back entrance to the apartment. The back entrance seemed like the best bet. But first, he had to move his car. It wouldn't be good for anyone to be able to identify him later because he'd parked his car near this place. Instead, he parked at a store a few blocks over and grabbed the lock box before he ran back over to the apartment. The cover of night was an asset for him and he got to the back door with no problem. Good thing this wasn't a higher end of town. He let himself into the apartment with only a single kick to the door, which was painfully easy to kick in without a whole lot of noise. Clearly the landlord was cheap, but that made his life easier tonight. Then again, a door couldn't stand in his way no matter how strong it was. Once inside, it was time to look around. This Xavier guy wasn't what he'd seemed at first. If he was the guy who'd shot Josh and shot up Brian's house, then he clearly knew far too much about Landon. Hopefully something here would clear that up for him.

There weren't any pictures on the walls or in the living room, which was as far as he'd gone the one time he'd been here. The guy was a jump off, and jump offs didn't get quality time with him. They got dick and then he moved on. It was that simple. Perhaps he should change that policy if ever he found himself in that situation again.

He went into the bedroom and found no pictures on the walls or anywhere easily identifiable. He went through the dresser drawers, looking for anything that could identify this guy. The guy didn't have any papers or pictures or anything else that would help him. So why was he after him? Was he just a creepy stalker? He'd find out soon enough, damn it.

He went through the house and found the fuse box, turning everything off. It was pitch black in the apartment, but he worked well in the dark. Now he just had to sit and wait.

About an hour later, the front door finally opened. Landon listened carefully, needing to make sure the man was alone. Only one set of footsteps walked across the floor to flick the light switch.

"What the hell?" he heard Xavier growl.

Landon smirked. Nothing like coming in to find that your lights don't work. Too bad that wasn't all he was going to find. He listened as Xavier went through the house, trying all the lights. He briefly wondered how long it would take the idiot to try flipping the fuses back on. Knowing the man was approaching his bedroom, Landon hid beside the door and out of view. When Xavier flipped the switches to restore the lights, he crouched down slightly. He was standing next to a dresser with a large mirror on the back of it, so it'd be hard to spot him. When Xavier walked through the bedroom door, he made his move.

Landon caught the man by the shirt collar with both hands, startling him and not wasting a second before tossing him violently into the dresser. He heard the mirror shatter as Xavier's frame crashed into it but caught him before he fell. Holding him by the throat with his right hand and restraining his right arm, he held him against the broken mirror and watched the recognition come over the man's face, followed by the intense hatred which made little to no sense.

"So, are you a stalker that's just off your fucking rocker, or is there a point to what you've been doing?" Landon squeezed to cut off his air. "I have to tell you that this definitely doesn't make you attractive to me. Trying to kill my old friend, my boyfriend and my family members kind of pisses me off." Landon tossed him across the room to the floor.

Xavier coughed as he sucked air back into his lungs, not that it would last long as Landon kicked him in the gut.

"Feel free to answer me anytime." Landon kicked him again.

"Wait, you've got it all wrong," Xavier gasped.

Landon rolled his eyes and kicked him again. "I recognized the car, dumb ass. This means you've been watching me for a while. So either you know something about my past or you're a stalker. Which is it?" Another kicked forced a pained cry from the other man. "Funny, this looks something like what I did to my first stalker. Only you're still breathing. Shall I change that?"

Xavier rolled away from him, trying to separate himself from his attacker but there wasn't much space to put between them. Landon yanked him off the floor with surprising strength and slammed him against the wall.

"So, are you going to tell me who you are, or am I just going to end you right here and now to save myself the stress and aggravation of dealing with you later?"

Xavier finally mustered some strength and shoved Landon backwards. Landon remained on his feet and braced himself, ready to knock the hell out of this guy.

"Doesn't feel so good to lose someone close to you, does it?" Xavier asked bitterly.

"If you think Josh was close to me you really need to check your sources," Landon shot back. "So what the hell was the point? What do you want?"

"What I want is for you to suffer," Xavier growled. "You take lives indiscriminately, don't you? It doesn't even bother you."

"You sound like a lunatic. What the actual fuck are you talking about?"

At this point, Xavier actually laughed. "You don't remember me at all, do you? I suppose you wouldn't. I'm three years younger than you."

"It's like you want me to rearrange your face. Who the hell are you really?" Landon demanded.

"I'm Shell's little cousin. I guess it's been so long since you hung around her that you wouldn't remember me."

Landon's face hardened, effectively hiding his surprise. "So you're Shell's cousin. That doesn't explain a damn thing."

"You're the reason she's dead, you and that little bastard Josh. And you got away with it. There's no one looking into her case. I can't figure out how in the hell you did it but no one even glanced your way when it's obvious that both of you had something to do with it."

Landon raised an eyebrow. "You weren't there when she died. How would you know who had anything to do with it?"

"I'm not stupid. I knew what was going on with my big cousin. I knew she kept messing with you even while she was with him. I knew you never had any intention of getting back with her and you just led her on. You led her right to her death. That's unforgiveable to me."

"Funny, I'm not looking for forgiveness. And frankly, I have more than just Shell in my past to worry about. But you don't know any of the facts. You just decided to play vigilante. So why approach me the way you did? You could have taken me out months ago. Why not just do it and get it over with?" Landon watched as the man's eye twitched. "Don't tell me you actually have a thing for me? That's rather creepy."

"Shut up!" Xavier shouted. "I did what I had to in order to get close to you. It wasn't enough to kill you. You had to suffer. I wanted you to watch everyone close to you die. You needed to feel my pain."

"Oh yeah, because it was so easy for me to deal with Shell being dead," Landon replied with obvious sarcasm. "Listen here, jackass, I did what I had to do in a situation I wish I'd never been in. You can blame me all you want, but this shit won't bring her back. You're dragging innocents into a situation they'd never have had to know about if not for you. At least Shell had an idea of what she was involved in. She knew me and Josh. She knew our tempers, and she knew if we got caught there'd be a fight."

"You don't get to just blame her for your actions. You killed her. I know it was you. I'll bet you're the one that pulled the trigger."

"Shows what the fuck you know. I like knives better." Landon smirked humorlessly. "The police ruled it the result of a drive-by shooting. Why exactly are you after me?"

"You and I both know it's a lie. I don't know who you fucked to get them to cover that bullshit for you, but I know better. It was you that killed her."

Landon shrugged. "Think what you want. It's not like it'll matter after today."

Xavier sneered at him. "Why? Are you going to kill me too?"

"Yeah probably, just seems like a much easier way to deal with it and keep my family safe from your insanity."

Xavier rushed him, tackling him to the floor. Landon grunted as his back hit the floor but managed to flip the other man off him. Scrambling back to his feet, he met Xavier getting up with a right hook to the jaw that kept the man down. Not content there, Landon rained down the blows, forcing Xavier to cover up. That is, until Xavier grabbed his fist and bit his arm.

"Son of a bitch!" he swore as he jerked his arm away.

Unfortunately, Xavier took a nice bit of skin off with that move and the blood flowed freely. In retaliation, Landon threw a left uppercut that knocked the man flat on his back. Xavier's teeth were rattled on that one and Landon shook his hurting left hand out of reflex. That wasn't his leading hand and he wasn't used to using it but desperate times called for desperate measures. Too bad Xavier didn't have a glass jaw and was already getting up and coming at him again.

"Fuck!" he swore as he realized he was already getting sluggish. Xavier tackled him right into the dresser, which broke under their combined weight. Moving no longer an option, Landon began to wonder if he was actually going to make it out of this situation for the first time.

Chapter Twenty-Six

Kevin wasn't willing to sit and wait on Landon. He'd called his phone so many times he'd lost count and Landon hadn't answered. He had no idea where to start looking for him and that pissed him off more. Why couldn't Landon have at least waited for him? The man insisted on handling everything on his own. It was as if he didn't know how to let someone help him.

Then again, how much help would he be? Kevin was no stranger to violence, but Landon seemed a lot more familiar than he'd thought. He knew Landon had a temper, and now he knew Landon had some parts of his past he never mentioned, but the changes he'd seen just over the past few weeks were mind blowing. He was used to being the protector, but he couldn't do that with Landon. Landon was very much his own man and nothing Kevin did could make him slow down or change. He just had to roll with it and hope that Landon came back unhurt. The question was, if Landon did what he sounded like he was going to do, could he stay with him and keep his secret? Kevin was far out of his element here, and not just because he was in love for the first time in his life with a man. He was in love with a man with a dark side and a past he'd never know in its entirety.

The door to his room opened and Renee walked in. She smiled at him as she sat next to him.

"You look tired," she told him.

"I am tired, and I'm worried," he replied.

"About Landon, right?"

He nodded. "I can't reach him. I'm sure you know what happened."

"Yeah the person in the dark car and the shooting. He told me all about it." Renee took his good hand in her own. "You have to get used to this with him, I'm afraid. He's never going to tell you more than he has to about the darker things in his past. And he's always going to try to do things on his own. All you can do in cases like this is wait because he'll always find a way to do it without you."

Kevin looked at her curiously. "How much do you know?"

"I don't know everything, but I know a lot because I've been his friend for so long."

"No, how much do you know about this situation?" Kevin asked. "Do you know where he went?"

"Not exactly," she replied. "But I know who he's after. I can't really tell you though."

"Why the hell not?" Kevin demanded.

"Because if I tell you then I'd be telling you something that will probably hurt you and I'd rather not be the cause of that issue," Renee responded calmly. "Besides, you are in a hospital and your arm is in a sling. You can't really help him."

"You can't honestly think I won't do something to help the man I love. I want to know and I don't care if you think it will hurt me. I won't tell him what I know or how I found out, but tell me where he is or who he's with."

Renee bit her lip and tried one more tactic to avoid this. "Kevin, you're not going to be released from the hospital yet."

"The hell I'm not. It's a gunshot wound and it's not that damn serious. I'm ready to get out of here and I want my man with me and in one piece. Now tell me what you know."

Renee sighed. "I'll tell you, but remember, you and Landon were broken up."

Landon realized quickly that something was wrong. Xavier was a human. Even before the king had released more of his power he'd never truly struggled in a fight before. When he suddenly went flying across the room, understanding dawned. The energy coming from the other man was not human. Xavier himself was human, but he had help from someone who most certainly was not human. Memories flashed through his mind of his past life as he struggled back to his feet. The glamour dropped from around him right before a searing pain shot through his left leg. He dropped to one knee and more pain seared through his left shoulder. He soon found himself staring up into the silencer on the end of a gun. Xavier paused as he looked down at him.

"What the hell are you?" he asked in something between wonder and fear.

Light emanated from Landon's eyes as he forced his power outward, sending the human flying across the room. When Xavier looked up from where he'd fallen against the wall, he could see a strange blue light surrounding Landon, almost like fire. The same emotions warred on the human's face as Landon stood up and limped towards him.

"Goddamn humans, always pulling off such cowardly acts. Didn't your confidante tell you who the hell you were fucking with?" Landon extended his hand and his power caught Xavier and as he lifted his hand, the human male was lifted off the floor and held in the air. "I'm done paying for mistakes of the past. If you want to come for me, you'd best be prepared for the consequences."

"You're not human either. What are you?"

Landon cocked his head to the side. "I'm the same thing as the person who put you up to this. I'm far older than I seem, and yet as young as you think I am. My kind predates humanity. You have long since called us by many names. Witches, wizards, gods, angels, demons. I am a Magus, which you only get to know because you will very shortly be dead."

Xavier struggled, flailing about in the air. It was a futile effort, but an all too human one. Landon held out his hand and the lock box appeared in it. It sprang open, seemingly on its own as far as Xavier could see. Inside was another gun, an all too familiar one to Landon. It was a .40 caliber handgun, with a silencer, and one human authorities would love to get their hands on. Landon flicked the wrist of his free hand and Xavier hit the wall again and fell to the floor, held down this time.

"Do you know where you actually fucked up at?" Landon asked coldly. "It wasn't that you messed with me. It's not that you shot at me twice. It's that you went after others that belong to me. So, I'll give you a chance. Tell me who the hell sent you after me and I won't force you to put this gun to your head and blow your own brains out. In case you're wondering, this is the gun that killed Shell. I've held onto it ever since her death."

"Bastard!" Xavier spat.

"Though I did not fire it, I played my part in your cousin's death. I pay for that daily. And if I had no one in this world depending on me, I might have let you get whatever revenge you deemed necessary on me. But I do have people I care for, people that care for me. And I cannot die here. It won't bring her back. Nothing I can do will bring her back. What I can do is remove your memory of me and what you now know and allow you to live in peace. Or I can kill you. And after what you've done, I won't hesitate to do it if you don't tell me what I want to know." Landon took the gun out of the lock box and with his power, sent it across the room and forced Xavier to take hold of it and put it to his head. "What's it going to be, human?"

"You know who she is. She said she's your stepmother."

Landon scowled and waved his hand, rendering Xavier unconscious. Behind him, he heard female laughter. He turned to come face to face with one Magus woman he wished had died long before.

"Levana." He spat the name, as repulsed as ever by her mere existence.

"How quaint. You do remember me." The unnaturally beautiful woman smiled back at him, but behind it was the madness of a Magus with far too much power. Her lips were a bright red and her eyes matched. Her skin was pale and she was thin, with high, defined cheekbones. Her hair was black, he knew, but she had it pinned underneath a crown. She dressed in a long black flowing gown and in her hand was a black staff with a green orb at the top of it.

"Only from my nightmares," Landon replied, preparing himself for the attack he was sure would come. "I know you and your perversions all too well."

Levana laughed, a feminine and crazed laugh that threatened to send Landon into a rage. "Oh come now, you still call them that. All of these centuries have gone by and you haven't changed. You enjoyed what I did to you."

"I was a child, you sick bitch!" Landon shot back.

Levana shrugged. "Are Magi ever really children? You were a spoiled little brat and you needed to be taught to obey. And now here you are as the result of a curse. You're not even at half of your full strength. This human body weakens you."

"I have more than enough power to murder you." Landon's hair began to blow around him as he gathered himself to attack the woman with everything he had.

"So that's how we have to do this?" Levana pointed the staff at him. "Then allow me to show you why you will always be inferior."

Chapter Twenty-Seven

Being the king had its advantages. Damien walked into Kevin's hospital room rather brazenly. Kevin had no clue who he was, and neither did Renee.

"Listen here, kids, I don't have a lot of time and neither do you. Would you like to know where Landon is?"

Kevin eyed him suspiciously. "Who are you?"

Damien scowled. "Someone that knows Landon far better than you. I'm also Brian's father, if you need a bit more of a direct answer. Now, do you want to help Landon or not?"

"He's not exactly in any condition to help him," Renee stepped in before Kevin could respond. "He was shot just yesterday."

"Mortals give me migraines. Answer the question, do you want to help him or not?" Damien wasn't used to resistance, even from mortals.

"Where is he?" Kevin asked.

"I can take you to him, but there are some things you need to know. I know all the things Landon hides from you, and some of them are quite essential for you to know in order to help him."

"What can you possibly know that we don't?" Kevin demanded.

"I suppose the only way to deal with this is to show you." Damien held out a hand and the door slammed shut and locked while the blinds closed. His glamour dropped and as his true beauty became evident, he was the primary source of light in the dimly lit room. He waved his hand again and the two humans found themselves silenced.

"The last thing I need is for you humans to run screaming when we have so little time to help Landon. Now, allow me to answer the most obvious question here. This is the true form of a Magus King. As you can see, it can be overwhelming for you humans, which is why we normally tone it down for you. Landon is also a Magus and originally the most lethal warrior I've ever had." Damien closed his eyes and cast the glamour again, also releasing the two to speak. "I'm sure you have a ton of questions and while nothing would amuse me more than answering them, we don't have the time. You need to get to Landon and I'm here to help."

"Why can't you just help him?" Renee asked irritably, rubbing her throat.

"Magus politics are complicated. Suffice it to say, I can't intervene directly. I need you to do so for me." Damien looked over Kevin. "I specifically need you to do it. So, let's see what I can do about that wound of yours."

Brian had an uneasy feeling and he hated being in the room with his family with nowhere else to go. A knock at the door at least gave him a welcome distraction.

"Dad? What are you doing here?"

Damien smiled. "There are things we need to talk about, son. You may not be happy with me once I tell you but given the circumstances, it's about time for you to find out."

Denise looked up from where she sat. "Let your father in, Brian."

Brian stepped aside and his father walked in. He closed the door behind him and watched as his father looked around the room.

"There seems to be one missing. Where is Paul? I feel the urge to speak with him." Damien's voice was calm, but Brian had the distinct feeling that there was a threat underneath it.

"He's at his mother's," Denise told him. "I assume you've decided it's time to tell Brian the truth so why don't you just focus on that?"

Damien smirked. "I'll just pay your husband a visit later." He turned to Brian. "Son, you might want to have a seat. It's about time you learn what I really am, and what you are, as well as how I know Landon far better than any of you."

Landon couldn't see a thing. He had no idea where he was. He tried moving his arms and found them tied down. This felt eerily similar to his nightmares. Then again, given the dreadful bitch he'd been fighting, she'd done this on purpose. She was the source of those nightmares after all.

"You're so dreadfully boring in this life," Levana's deceptively seductive voice broke the silence.

"Don't you know how to just lay down and die?" Landon bit out. "You'd be doing the world a favor."

Levana laughed. "And leave you with no one to torment you constantly? I think not. There's much that you have to suffer for."

"You know if you don't kill me, I'm going to kill you. There's not a power on any plane that can stop me." Landon opened his eyes to find her standing in front of him. "But that's why you came at me now, while I still only have a portion of my memories and power."

"That would imply that I fear you. I don't fear you any more than I fear that wretched king of yours. But I wonder if you know the answer to my question. Why do you continue to serve a master who is so much weaker than you?"

"Why do you continue to be such a useless cunt?" Landon sneered at her.

The Magus woman slapped him, splitting his lip. In turn, Landon spat blood in her face.

"You always were a disgusting, foul mouthed little creature." Levana turned away from him.

"And you were always a raging, psychotic bitch." He couldn't hold the retorts back if he tried. "So, what's the plan? More torture until I break free and wreck your fucking face, or are you actually going to kill me? You'd better decide quickly."

Levana laughed. "There's no fear of you breaking free. Those little threads binding you will sap any Magus energy. And when your king comes to rescue you, he will be caught in the same thing. You see, this isn't all about you. I've decided that Avalon's throne should be mine. If I kill you both, it becomes mine."

Landon laughed. "You are an idiot. You're not in line for the throne. Did you think Damien had no heir?"

"His heir will be dealt with. A show of force will make anyone bend to my will. Who's going to stop me?"

Landon looked around him, noting that they were still in Xavier's apartment. "What did you do with the human?"

"He's a pawn that I can blame all of this death on for the humans. Not that it'll matter. Once I take control of Avalon I think I'll take the human realm too. Might as well rule the little beasts as well. And now, I think I'll leave you here to suffer as all your memories return. I hope one of them makes you hate the king."

She vanished with a maniacal laugh. She always had been dramatic. Landon looked around and sighed. He was suspended in the air and tied by his arms and legs in a splayed position. He was wounded in several places and couldn't tap into the slightest bit of energy. Worse, memories began to bombard him the moment Levana left him. Memories of his past life flooded back uncontrollably, leaving him unable to even contemplate his current situation.

Chapter Twenty Eight

Kevin couldn't say he wasn't scared. Though Damien had assured him that what Landon was didn't change who Kevin knew him as, there was that all too human fear of the unknown. He was outside Xavier's apartment and his thoughts were racing a mile a minute. On one hand, Landon was the man he loved. He'd known him for years. On the other hand, Kevin was in over his head. What would he walk in on, really? Was Landon in danger like the Magus King told him, or was this a part of a game? What if Landon was enjoying himself in there? Could he really walk in and be made a fool of?

Kevin shook his head and got out of the car. He wouldn't let his doubts prevent him from going in there. Damien said Landon was in trouble and he and Landon were together. Vaguely he wondered if that meant the same thing to a Magus warrior. He'd have to ask him once he got in there. He advanced forward and walked up the stairs to the apartment. He found the door unlocked and walked in. An unconscious man lay at an odd angle on the floor against the wall as he walked in, but that wasn't his concern. He closed the door behind him and walked through the dark apartment. In the center of the apartment, he found Landon suspended in the air, his head down and eyes closed. He was bleeding from the arm and leg as well as from his right side. His clothes were shredded and the sight of him made Kevin regret his hesitation to come in.

"Landon?" Kevin advanced slowly until he stood right in front of him. "Are you awake?"

"Unfortunately yes." Landon opened his eyes and the effect of his Magus heritage hit Kevin immediately like a punch to the gut, knocking the wind from him. "What exactly are you doing here?"

"Why aren't you surprised to see me?" Kevin countered, looking around him. "And how can I get you down?"

Landon raised his head to look at the wires holding him. "Shine the light from your phone around my hands. You should be able to see the wires holding me here. There's a knife tied at my back. Use it to cut them."

Kevin reached around him to get the knife first, then pulled out his phone and pressed a button to light it up. Shining the light near Landon's arms, he made a quick cut with the knife, severing the wires that held his left arm first. Landon slumped forward and hissed in pain. Kevin paused but Landon waved him on.

"Just get me down. I'll be fine when I get out of this."

Kevin stood directly in front of him, to make sure he could catch him as he cut his other arm free. Landon fell forward and Kevin caught him, managing to stay standing.

"Don't forget my legs," Landon told him.

Kevin lifted him onto his shoulder before cutting his legs free, making sure he wouldn't fall again. Landon chuckled.

"Are you really going to carry me around like a burlap sack?" he asked.

"Does it really matter as long as I get you out of here?" Kevin replied.

"Put me on my feet and just help me walk out. I'm not a complete invalid."

Kevin did as he asked, keeping his arm around his waist and throwing Landon's arm over his shoulder. Once at the door, they found Xavier was gone.

"Son of a bitch, I really need him not to be alive," Landon muttered.

"Why?" Kevin asked.

"I'll explain later. Let's get out of here."

Kevin continued on out of the door and down to his car. He put Landon in on the passenger's side as gently as he could manage before getting in on the driver's side. As he went to start the car, Landon placed a hand on his arm to stop him.

"Clearly we need to talk," he said quietly, his eyes searching Kevin for a reaction.

Kevin avoided looking at him. "We can talk when you're not bleeding heavily." He started the car and put it in gear, driving off quickly.

Landon sighed. "I don't need a hospital, if that's where you were thinking of going. Just go to my house."

Kevin glanced at him. "You're bleeding all over my seat. Why would I take you home?"

"Because in a few minutes the wounds will close on their own. Just do it Kevin, and then you can be as mad at me as you want."

Kevin clenched his jaw. "I'm not exactly mad at you. I don't know what I'm feeling right now."

"It's anger, mixed with resentment and pain," Landon told him. "I can sense your emotions rather clearly at the moment when I don't have my glamour on."

"Glamour?"

"What the Magi use to hide our true beauty from you. It tends to make humans desire us more than they should. It gets messy if you're in our presence too long." Landon closed his eyes. "Give me a few minutes and I'll put it back."

"I'd rather see the real you," Kevin told him. "I need to get used to this."

"Suit yourself." Landon didn't open his eyes, but his senses were open enough to sense all that Kevin felt at the moment. It wasn't going to be an easy night.

By the time they reached Landon's house, his wounds had closed and he was able to get out of the car and walk on his own. Upon entering the house, he wasn't surprised to see Damien sitting on his couch waiting.

"I'm a bit surprised at your methods this time," Landon told him.

Damien shrugged. "I wasn't about to fall into Levana's trap. It's become obvious recently that she's intent on gaining more power. Your father can no longer contain her."

"Would have been nice if you had clued me in," Landon muttered.

"I had to be sure it was her. Now I am." Damien's eyes held a glint of mischief. "There is a surprise waiting for you in your room."

"I'd hardly call your pissed off son a surprise. I can sense him just fine. I always have been able to and I'm well aware of what I'm walking into." Landon turned to Kevin. "Do me a favor and wait in here. I'll be out in a second."

Kevin glared at him but made no response. Landon sighed and went into his room, finding Brian sitting on his bed. Landon stopped a few feet away.

"So, you know the truth and you're pissed at me, right?"

"It's not the fact that we are what we are that pisses me off. It's the fact that you're only here looking after me because you have to."

Landon raised an eyebrow. "Did your father tell you that?"

"He told me he assigned you as my guardian," Brian replied.

"So you're simply assuming that I don't care because your father has me guarding you?" Landon almost laughed. "Kid, you're being really stupid right now. I have been in this life longer than you've been alive. I was sent here as a punishment. Your father said I was too brutal, too cold and unfeeling. He said some time as a human might change my perspective. Guarding you was an extra add on, one I didn't mind taking on."

Brian simply glared at him, so Landon sat on the bed next to him and wrapped an arm around him.

"You're really just angry that I didn't tell you what I know. I didn't tell you what I am and what you are, and I didn't tell you what your father really was. Unfortunately, I wasn't allowed to. There are a lot of things about being a Magus that are strange to humans, but it works for us. It's how we've lived so long and separated ourselves from them. Your father simply has a taste for human women."

Brian really wanted to be angry, but he never could stay angry with Landon. "I hate not being included. And I've been so bitter towards my dad for so long. This is a lot to process."

"Well, I hate to be the bearer of bad news, but I'm pretty sure there's more to tell. Go in the living room and wait for me."

Brian stood and did as he was told, giving Landon a moment to himself. He rose and looked in the mirror, noting that his glamour was definitely back in place. Brown eyes stared back at him and he didn't have that otherworldly beauty about him. Not that he was bad on the eyes but being in his Magus glory was a bit much while in the human world. He changed his clothes and headed back out, finding that Renee had joined the group.

"I take it your memories have returned entirely?" Damien asked.

Landon nodded. "Yeah, although I don't understand why she would let them."

"She was hoping that you were unreasonable, I assume. Apparently she didn't realize I couldn't bind your powers and reincarnate you into the mortal world without your agreement." Damien chuckled. "I look forward to when she fights you at full strength again."

"You're talking over our head here and I, for one, would love to know what the hell is going on," Kevin interrupted.

Damien's amusement was evident. "There's no need to hide much from you at this point. You've seen us in our full glory. Well, you've seen me. Landon looks quite different in Magus armor with a sword in hand. He's a sight to behold on the battlefield."

Landon rolled his eyes and took a seat in an armchair, facing everyone else. "Not everyone shares your bloodlust. I'd scare the hell out of them, assuming I haven't scared them already."

Kevin was staring at his lover, clearly wanting him to speak. "Must you glare at me like that?" Landon asked him.

"I'm not glaring. I'm waiting," Kevin responded.

Landon sighed. "What you already know about me is still as true as it was yesterday. There's simply more to it. Unlike most humans, if Magi die and are reincarnated, we can retain the memories of our past life. My past life is what you need to know a bit more about."

Damien elected to take over here. "We are quite a bit older than you might think. The Magi don't age after a certain point in life. Normally around the age of twenty-five, we stop. We are a society that operates based around power. The most powerful rule. My family was born to the throne of Avalon, but each heir must earn the throne. I've ruled for a very long time without producing an heir, until Brian that is."

"The heir can choose a champion, however," Landon continued. "I am Damien's champion. When his father died, he wasn't very experienced in battle. My family has always sworn allegiance to the Adaire family. I took up the task of securing the throne for him, and I did so without mercy."

"You said that you were sent here as a punishment. What did you do?" Brian asked.

"I lost my lover," Landon replied. "About three hundred years ago, he was killed in battle. Afterwards, all I knew how to do was to fight. Every skirmish, every potential uprising against the crown, I met with force. Across Avalon, my name was spoken with fear. I was the merciless right hand of the king. They say my power is unrivaled and my efficiency on the battlefield only got better once I lost my lover. I felt no real desire to continue on. Shutting down my feelings was easier. I was cast into this life because I elected to execute a human."

"The human was a thief, but many of the Magi love to steal from humans. His death was not warranted," Damien added.

"He pissed me off. That was all the warranting I needed," Landon replied. "However, I was a bit too caught up in the bloodlust, so Damien decided I needed to live as a human. Unfortunately, the violence spilled over into this life several times. I have almost as many human enemies as I do Magus. I'm a dark natured person. So much of what I do is done in the shadows that the shadows are an extension of me. I hold a lot more secrets than this within me."

"What I want to know is what the hell happened at that apartment?" Kevin demanded.

Renee and Brian both looked uneasy at his tone. Damien looked amused and Landon's jaw ticked in obvious irritation.

"I went there to settle it. I figured out where I'd seen the car before. I went there to silence him. That was easier said than done when not at full power while he was backed by a Magus. Plus, he shot me twice. Once she overpowered and then restrained me, well, you saw the result." Landon scowled. "That bitch hasn't been able to overpower me in centuries."

"It's so weird to hear you say that," Renee muttered.

"Sorry. I'd have loved to have told you, but part of my punishment was not to have my memories." Landon smiled at her. "I did need a friend while I was here and you've been the best at it."

Renee waived that off. "I'm no stranger to the supernatural. You know that. I just never knew you were a Magus. I guess I should have though."

"What about all the past relationships?" Kevin asked. "Was that in this life or the last one?"

"This life," Damien answered. "Love is something none of us can defend against. It is the fall of man and Magi alike. I watched and hated it, but he had to get the full experience again."

"In other words, just because I am a Magus doesn't mean my feelings for anyone changes," Landon told him. "As far as my personality goes, you know me just as well now as before. It's just that as a Magus, I'm really a bit more extreme in some ways than what you've seen from me."

"At least he has refrained from outright slaughters," Damien commented.

"I'm not done yet and you know it," Landon told him. "Something has to be done about Xavier, and then Levana is mine to do with as I wish. You agreed I could handle this however I deemed necessary."

Damien nodded in confirmation. "My word is binding. The situation is yours to handle."

Landon smirked. "Good, then I intend to. I probably won't be able to catch up to her here, but I can damn sure fix him."

"Yes, and while you do that, I have another little pest to have a conversation with." Damien vanished, causing everyone else in the room to jump in surprise.

"Can you do that?" Kevin asked Landon.

Landon smirked. "Yes, I can. I probably wouldn't because I'm used to using normal means to get around these days, but I can."

"You know, this makes an odd amount of sense. It explains how you got away with the whole Shell thing, and the excessive amount of strength you display every now and then." Renee smiled at him. "So, you're a witch, huh?"

Brian laughed while Landon scowled.

"I'm not a witch. That's the term for humans that learn magic, like yourself. I was born with my magic." Landon looked at Kevin, who wasn't joining in on the jokes. "So, do we need to talk or what?"

Kevin shrugged. "Maybe we do."

Renee looked back and forth between the two. "Should we leave?"

"I guess we could use the time alone. Kevin has some things to get off his chest that he won't say in front of you two." Landon's eyes didn't leave Kevin's.

"Well, Brian, let's go. I don't know if they're pissed at each other or really just want to jump each other's bones, but I'd rather not wait around to find out."

Brian snorted and followed her out. When the door closed behind them, there was only silence between the two. Landon chose to break it.

"If you're going to freak out and dump me, now's the time."

"I want to see you," Kevin told him.

"Come again?" Landon wasn't sure he understood him.

"Damien said I didn't see you in your full glory. I want to see you," Kevin repeated.

Landon sighed. "Kevin, I'm not sure it's the best idea in the world to repeatedly reveal myself in front of you. I don't want you to turn into someone who's more obsessed with me than in love with me."

"I don't think you get to make that call. You being a Magus warrior doesn't bother me nearly as much as...." Kevin stopped.

"Not telling you that Xavier made a pass at me," Landon finished for him.

"Yeah, that. I figured you would mess around eventually when you got tired of me or while we weren't together. But you know, what bothers me most is just how much you keep from me. I hate being lied to."

Landon raised an eyebrow at him. "I didn't lie. I simply didn't tell you. I didn't tell you about Xavier because it meant nothing to me. As for me being a Magus, well, I couldn't exactly show you or prove it to you. Besides, there are rules in place to protect us from becoming general human knowledge again. We've discovered that it doesn't work out so well for us when humans know we exist and walk among them."

Kevin stood up and began to pace, obviously frustrated. Landon watched him, unable to get a clear read on his emotions.

"Kevin, come here," he ordered softly.

"I don't want to be that close to you right now. I'm pissed off," Kevin snapped back.

"I didn't ask you what you wanted. I told you to come over here."

Kevin stopped and glared at him. "So now you think you can order me around, just because you're not..."

"Human," Landon finished for him again. "If I wanted to stress that fact, I wouldn't have told you to come here. I'd have forced you. I told you to come here because last I checked, we're still officially a couple and I want you here so that I can apologize."

Kevin waited several seconds to cave in and walk towards him. Landon rose to meet him and wrapped his arms around him in a tight embrace.

"I'm sorry I held so much from you. I'm sorry you found out the way you did, and I'm sorry I put you at risk because of my past actions. If you want to leave, I'll understand."

"If I leave, I know your secret. I don't get the feeling you'd really be able to just let me go."

Landon lay his head on Kevin's shoulder, not letting him go. "I would be allowed to let you go, but only after removing your memories of me entirely. If that's what you want, it can be done."

Kevin looked down at him and finally wrapped his arms around him as well with a sigh. "No, I don't want that. I don't want to forget you. I don't want to lose you."

Landon broke away enough to look up at him. "I'm not sure you understand what that will entail. I operate in ways you won't always agree with. I may have to leave for long periods of time and I can't take you with me. I'll always come back to you, and I don't feel the need to wander. I don't want anyone but you."

"I'll learn to deal with it. That's why I want to see you in your natural state. I don't want you to have to hold back from me at all."

Landon stepped back. "I'll do this for you now but don't count on it happening often. The glamour is made to protect humans, not us."

Kevin watched as the glamour fell, and Landon changed. Landon had always been attractive, but when he dropped that glamour, he looked other worldly. Deep blue eyes gazed out of a stunningly beautiful face. His cheekbones were higher and more pronounced, and there was suddenly a point to his ears.

"Do you change elsewhere?" Kevin heard himself ask, not meaning to ask the question aloud.

Landon responded by pulling his shirt off and dropping his pants. His body was better toned than before. In fact, one could say that his body was perfect. There were no blemishes of any sort on his skin. His body could have been chiseled out of stone. One thing remained the same, and that was the very noticeable erection he was currently sporting.

"There's no need to glamour that," Landon told him, a smile spreading over his face.

Kevin moved forward to touch him. He wasn't being sexual; he was simply reaffirming what his eyes saw. He looked into Landon's eyes, so different from the eyes he'd known for so long.

"If you insist on touching me everywhere, this is going to lead somewhere I don't think you want to go right now," Landon warned. "I know you're upset with me. I know you're hurt. I can feel it."

Kevin leaned down and kissed him. The kiss lacked all of his usual emotion.

"It's not fair for me to feel the way I do, but I do and I can't change it that easily," Kevin told him.

Landon exhaled and the glamour came over him again while he turned and redressed himself. "Then I'll give you time. You learned a lot today, none of which I intended for you to learn. But what's done is done."

Kevin advanced forward and wrapped his arms around him from behind. "We're not breaking up. That's not what I need or want. I want you with all my heart, Landon. I need you. I just need a moment to get past the fact that you went to someone else, even if we weren't together and it was all my fault."

"Don't try to act as if what I am doesn't bother you either," Landon told him. "I know it does on some level."

"It's not the way you think it is. My problem is just that we're so uneven in everything. You're comfortable with being out and I'm not. You don't hide that part of yourself at all. I want to give you so much more than what I've given you, but I can't."

"Sexuality is something that is generally very simple for my people." Landon stepped out of his embrace. "I understand now more than ever that that isn't the case in this world. It's not so simple for you because you weren't raised in a way that lets you feel truly free to be yourself. Your society has been caught up with their own preconceived notions of right and wrong for centuries. No matter what I am or how powerful I am, only you can take those steps towards truly being yourself."

Kevin hid a look of hurt. "So what are you saying?"

Landon turned back and gave a small smile. "I'm not ending anything, Kevin. If you still want me, then you have me. Everything is in your hands now."

He left the room, going into his bedroom and finally getting the chance to climb into bed after removing his clothes again. He'd only been in bed a few minutes before Kevin entered the room and stripped down. He climbed into bed with him and pulled him back into his embrace.

"I love you, Landon. I may not be the most open guy with that, and I'm sorry if that's something you need. I will work on that and anything else necessary to keep you."

"Just be yourself, Kevin. That's all I need you to do to be happy." Landon turned towards him and wrapped an arm around him. "I love you and I don't need you to do anything for me that makes you uncomfortable."

Kevin nodded and drew him close, kissing him once again. This kiss was tender, but at least some of his usual eagerness was there. Still, Landon broke the kiss and lay his head on his lover's chest. Sleep finally claimed him moments later.

Chapter Twenty-nine

F*lashback*
 Landon found himself chained against a hard surface. He struggled but was unable to escape. All too familiar maniacal laughter rang out. He cringed. The room was dark but he knew the walls. They were covered in blood. This was a torture chamber, and he'd been in it far too many times.

"Oh, you've been a naughty boy, haven't you?" Levana appeared before him, scantily dressed in a black leather bodice and heels. To the average man, she'd be attractive, maybe even gorgeous. Her body was exquisite. Not exceptionally thin, but not fat, she had the type of curves to make a mortal man drool. Her lips were painted with a bright red lipstick and her hair was down long.

Landon struggled anew, knowing it was no use. The bitch had him right where she wanted him, and he was powerless to fight her.

"Now, you know that there's no way out. I fail to see why you fight it so. You love our little sessions here, don't you?" A whip appeared in her hand and she put it to use, a single lash breaking the skin across Landon's chest. "You'll rise to the occasion shortly. You always do. Filthy little creature." She whipped him again and he gritted his teeth against the pain. She wanted him to cry out in pain and he refused to give her the satisfaction. The unfortunate thing was that the whip was laced with one of her potions, one designed to get his body to do what his heart and soul raged against.

"You know I'm going to kill you one day," he warned her, wincing as the whip came down again.

Levana laughed again. "Oh how wonderful. You still cling to that notion that you hate me. I will enjoy working you over for the rest of your days. You are my property, and you will serve me in all ways."

Landon ground his teeth as the potion worked its way through him. He hated it. No matter how much he worked against it, he could feel the effects. His dick was hardening and he saw that sick glint in her eyes. How the deranged whore had come up with her methods was something he'd probably never know. Unfortunately, he had no choice but to suffer through this, as he had so many times before.

Levana's clothes simply vanished. She walked towards him in a way she most assuredly thought was sexy and seductive. To Landon, she looked more like a female lion about to pounce on her prey, and that prey was him. To her credit, she didn't pounce. She had him restrained, held up in the air by threads around his wrists and ankles that sapped him of his power, leaving him a slave to her twisted designs. As he glared his hatred at her, she stepped towards him and climbed up to wrap her legs around his waist. He growled as she positioned herself so that the head of his dick was poised to enter her. She flashed that sadistic smile before impaling herself on him, letting out a groan. She tossed her head back and duck her nails into his back until she drew blood. She raked her nails across his back and he forced himself to keep quiet. She would not get the cry of pain she so desperately desired.

"So much better than the others. So strong and forceful." She sounded breathless as she rode him. "I will own you, now and always." Those haunting red eyes turned on him. "Always."

Modern day

Landon sat up as he jolted awake, sweat pouring down his face. He looked around his bedroom, his breath coming too quickly. His heart was racing and he found relief in Kevin's arms coming around his shoulders.

"What's wrong?" he asked, genuinely concerned.

Landon lowered his head. "It was a dream, or rather, a flashback. I don't normally have them when I'm with you."

Kevin brushed his lover's hair back from his face. "Do you want to tell me about it?"

Landon sighed. "Do you remember when I told you I had been a victim of sexual abuse when I was young?"

"Yeah, I remember." Kevin's voice conveyed the male equivalent of sympathy in such a situation, rage.

"The woman who bound me earlier is the perpetrator of that. It didn't occur in this life. It was in my original life, my young days as a Magus before I became a warrior. I wasn't always so dominating and forceful. I wasn't always strong enough to defend myself. She's the reason I became determined to be stronger. I excelled as a warrior because I wanted nothing more than to kill her and never to be her victim again."

Kevin rubbed his arms in a comforting gesture. "That's not really necessary is it? You won't be her victim again if you don't allow yourself to be."

"It doesn't work that way with her. Until the day she dies, she will continue to come after me. She will go after anyone

I care for. She killed the lover I told you about earlier. She'll come for you eventually."

"So what do you intend to do about it?" Kevin asked him.

Landon looked at him. "One way or another, this cycle between us has to end. The only way it ends is when one of us is dead."

"I know you're supposed to be this badass warrior, but I don't feel comfortable with you going off into dangerous situations alone. My instinct is to go with you."

Landon smiled. "That's sweet and all, but you can't be there for this one. What she brings to a fight is something you can't deal with. But I can."

"So what am I supposed to do, just sit here and wait while hoping you make it through this in one piece?"

"No, you're going to sleep and when you wake up, it'll be done." Landon flicked a hand at his face and Kevin slumped and fell back on the bed. With Kevin in a magically induced sleep, Landon stood up and left the house. No weapons were needed this time.

"You are a bit too headstrong."

Landon stopped and turned to Damien. "Are you going to help in some way or do I just get to go in as I am and slaughter her this way? One way or another, the bitch dies tonight."

Damien extended his hand. "I agree with you. But you'll need something first. There's one last seal on your power, one I can't release here. Come with me."

"I hate traveling with you." Landon placed his hand in the king's and the world went black.

Chapter Thirty

Landon came to in surroundings he'd only seen in dreams the past 25 years. He could feel the connection to the land. Avalon, his homeland. He felt better just standing in it. He looked out over green fields of his home and wondered where in the land Damien had brought him.

"Ah, I see at least one memory hasn't fully returned." Damien stood next to him. "We were a little old fashioned. Your power could not be fully contained by me. It's much too great. So we contained the rest in the way of our people, the way used in legend."

Landon raised an eyebrow. "You contained the rest of my power in a sword in a stone? Really? How cliche."

Damien chuckled. "If you weren't so powerful, it wouldn't have been so difficult. In fact, I had to use two swords. Since you remember that legend, you know the rest. It's up to you to draw the sword from the stone in front of the cliffs there."

"Yeah, but unlike the legends, this doesn't make me a king. Just the king's shadow."

"It's where you chose to be," Damien reminded him.

Landon smirked. "Never regretted it either. The whole king thing works better for you than it would for me. Now, let's see if I can get this sword."

Landon walked forward alone, towards the cliffs in the distance. He let his power flare out and connect to his homeland, a long shadow being cast behind him. Reaching the foot of the plateau, he found one large stone with two swords sticking out of it. Both were straight swords with jet black hilts and small gold pommels. The blades were relatively thin but strong and glinted in the light. The guards were almost nondescript, being just big enough to prevent his hand from slipping up to the blade. He reached forward and grasped the hilt of one, only for the ground to shake slightly. He looked up at the plateau and saw a face in it. The land was often alive in Avalon and this was an ancient being.

"So you've come at last to retrieve your swords? I hope you have learned from your time as a human."

"I've learned a great deal, old one, but now is the time to use my power again for the benefit of Avalon as well as the human world," Landon replied.

The old one laughed, a deep rumble that shook the ground again. "Fighting for the benefit of the human world? I daresay you have learned a great deal. Go now and be whole once again. I look forward to seeing how you progress from here. The old ones are always watching."

Landon drew the swords from the stone with ease, recognizing that it was only because the old one had released them. One sword was shorter than the other, noticeably so after being drawn from the stone. Power flooded back into him, temporarily overwhelming him. His glamour shattered, his true form now all the more glorious in his homeland. Sheaths were now strapped to his waist, so he sheathed the swords and turned to see Damien standing next to him.

"You do have other weapons, you know. You always preferred knives and swords to long range weapons."

Landon turned his blue eyes to the king. "It's been far too long since I've been here. But you know I can't stay, even after she's dead. Not now." His voice was slightly deeper with a lilt to it that only the Magi possessed. There was power behind his voice.

"Yes, you do have people in your human life that love you. I do not need you to rush back here. Things are well in hand." Damien smiled. "My son loves you more than he loves me, I'm sad to say. And he'll need you to teach him and prepare him. One day, even I must step aside."

"Yes, but that one day is not today. Today, I get rid of yet another threat to your throne. With my power restored, her death is assured."

"I'm not so worried about the throne. I have every confidence that she would fail in that regard. Don't make this about me. This is your revenge, your vengeance."

Landon smiled. "Times like this you'd almost be doable. Don't get your hopes up. I'm quite happy with Kevin and I promised to come back to him, but right now you seem like less of an ass."

Damien shook his head with a grin. "Only you can speak to me in such a way."

"It helps to be your champion. Now, I'd better get to the task at hand. I can't hold Kevin under forever and he's going to be pissed. So I need to get this done so that I can make it up to him." Landon gathered his power, envisioning the hellhole he never wanted to return to but had to in order to finally kill that horrid woman. He vanished as Damien looked off into the distance.

"Good luck, old friend," he whispered.

Chapter Thirty-One

Landon knew this place all too well. It had been his family's land at one point. He'd left and never come back, never satisfied that he could do what needed to be done. It had been a vibrant place once. Now it was dreary and lifeless. The ground was cold and barren. The walls of the manor he should call home were dark and uninviting. He growled low in his throat as he looked around the courtyard.

He felt the ripple of power alerting Levana to his presence. Now the fun would begin.

Armed soldiers poured out of the manor. The Magi moved at unnatural speeds, but Landon was no ordinary Magus. His blue eyes brightened as he prepared to go all out for the first time in years. His body remembered it all. He sprang forward, his speed surpassing that of the soldiers he faced. Electing not to draw his sword, as these soldiers were doing what they were supposed to in following the reigning head of the family, he struck out and his fists caught two soldiers in the face. Before those two fell, he was off. His body remembered the old skills before his mind, and that was just fine. Faster than any human or Magus, he shot through their ranks, striking out with force that would be lethal to any human. Technically, the force he used was lethal to several of the soldiers, or at the very least incapacitating. The soldiers dropped before many of them could even see him. Several seconds later, after several dozen had fallen, they caught a blur of movement. Landon stopped and pivoted on one foot, his hair swinging around him, before dashing off into the midst of other soldiers.

Howls of pain filled the air and the sky darkened. Flashes of light sprang up through the soldiers, the impact of Landon's armored fists or feet striking the armored bodies of the soldiers he was currently assaulting. Bones cracked and snapped, as the lethal warrior that Landon was didn't allow him to hold back. Eventually he sprang up the stairs and kicked open the large oak door of the manor, actually taking them off the hinges. More soldiers awaited him, and he vaguely wondered just how much the army had grown under Levana. His father had never felt the need for that many soldiers around him.

His speed overwhelming the soldiers, he dashed up the stairs and finally stopped, looking down at the soldiers who had flooded the ground level.

"Sorry, boys, but the lord of the manor is home, and I don't have time to fool around with you." He waved his hand and a wave of white-hot energy spread through the ground level, leveling the Magus soldiers below, and destroying most of the level as well. He smirked, satisfied with that result, and moved on through the top floor.

"So much stronger than you were before." Levana appeared in his path, her staff in hand, forcing him to stop. "I could do great things with you."

"I'd much rather you die and burn in whatever hell exists after this life." Landon threw his hands up and his power flew from him, slamming into the woman before him and sending her flying down the hall. Exerting her own power, Levana brought herself to a halt in midair and her gaze suddenly turned cold.

"Naughty boy, you don't strike out at your master. Now I'm going to have to bring you to heel."

The light in the room began to fade, though Landon's blue eyes were very clearly seen. Where Levana's gaze was cold, Landon's was a blazing inferno. In the growing darkness, they were cold blue flames.

"Clearly you've been trapped in your own world so much that you don't know who and what I am." In the dim light, Landon's smile, totally lacking any warmth or amusement, could just barely be seen. "I am one with the darkness. I live in the shadows. You are nothing more than a deluded, pathetic little woman who should have been killed long ago. You are the whore who seduced your way into my father's heart. You are the bane of my existence. You are the largest shadow from my past. You are what children fear to find under their beds in the dark. You created an absolute monster, a living breathing weapon incapable of mercy or forgiveness."

"Are you saying that I made you?" Levana laughed. "All I did was make you a man."

"You made me a victim, and now I will return the favor. But this time, my dick isn't what will impale you. This time, all you get from me is cold, hard steel. You will bleed, you will suffer, and you will know pain." Landon drew one of the swords at his waist. "I'm going to enjoy showing you the weapon you forged, the weapon that forever stands against you. But forever won't be so very long for you."

In the ever-growing darkness, Landon attacked. His body once again knew what to do by instinct. Levana was no helpless maiden. When his sword swung in a deadly arc for her head, her staff blocked it. Landon didn't miss a beat. He knew exactly what she was capable of. He'd been tortured by her for years in his early life. As such, he kept fighting, the sword glinting in the darkness as the two swung and parried back and forth. Landon didn't show signs of strain. His old skill hadn't diminished. Spotting an opening, he moved his sword in a circle and caught the staff in the center, flicking his wrist up to disarm his foe. He kicked her harshly in the chest and delighted as he watched her go flying through a door at the end of the hall. A second later, a ball of green light, pure burning energy, came flying at him. To the shock of its creator, Landon reached out and caught it, holding it before him the way one might hold a baseball prior to a pitch.

"Poor Levana. You really don't understand that the king's champion does not fall so easily." Landon's eyes glowed brighter as he channeled his own power into the ball of energy he held. "Now you get to see how I secured his throne for him firsthand. This might hurt."

He grinned as he hurled the ball back at her, and a wave of bright green energy filled the hallway before slamming into her and destroying the walls around them. The foundation of the building was rocked and windows shattered.

At the top of a hill several feet away, Damien watched the brilliant colors of energy destroying Landon's childhood home. He sighed.

"I didn't intend for you to wreck the place. I'll never understand why you can't kill one of your own kind without destroying everything in sight. It's not that difficult really."

Do you always talk to yourself? Landon's voice came to him.

Damien smiled. "Oh, I knew you could hear me. You're overdoing it. This is your home, after all. Your direct tie to the land."

The land is my home, not this torture chamber. I want it gone and you're not exactly in a position to stop me now, are you?

"Valid point," Damien conceded. "But your spell on Kevin won't last much longer. When the light of the sun hits his face in the mortal world, he will awaken. Don't you think you should finish this before that happens?"

You're meddling. I didn't cast it for him to awaken before I was good and damn ready.

"King's prerogative." Damien gave two quick claps. "Chop, chop. Let's wrap this up."

Jackass.

Damien watched as the manor exploded, rubble flying in every direction. He flicked his wrist, projecting a barrier to protect himself from the flying debris.

"It may be a bit overboard, but it's always interesting to watch him in action," he mumbled to himself.

Landon stood in the midst of the fire, untouched by it. He'd created it, after all, and his power formed a shield around him. Levana was alive, moving among the flames. She'd blended in with the fire, attempting to surprise him. She still didn't understand. He turned in a direction where he knew she wouldn't be and flicked his hand, sending a wave of his power to put out part of the fire. As he'd expected, he'd drawn her out. As she rose up behind him, her body jerked, and she stopped. Landon snorted.

"I can't believe you fell for that. I didn't become Damien's champion by luck. I slaughtered his enemies without remorse."

Landon's hand was on the hilt of his sword, the blade of which was currently in Levana's chest. "Didn't you hear the stories? I bring death as if I am death itself. You never know until your soul is ready to depart from your body."

He stepped forward and turned, pulling the sword from her chest and without switching his grip swung the sword and decollated the wicked Magus woman. Her body fell and her head hit the ground seconds later. He stared down at her for several seconds, watching as her blood flowed out on the ground. Finally, he turned and the flames washed over her body as he walked away. He stopped at the edge of the property and turned back.

"It's time for you to leave. Kevin will awaken shortly." Damien stood beside him again.

"Believe me, I'd rather be there than here. But at least I'll put out the fire." Landon waved his hand over the scene in front of him and the flames died out, revealing only rubble where the manor used to be.

"You do realize that your father still lives and will probably be upset that you've destroyed the family home?" Damien questioned.

"You do realize that I don't give a flying fuck what he thinks, don't you?" Landon countered. "If he has an issue, he can certainly bring it to me, and he can join his bitch in hell. Now send me home."

"Very well. But remember, your work for me is far from done."

Chapter Thirty-Two

Arriving at home, Landon entered his bedroom and his clothes dissolved, leaving him naked. He climbed into bed and pulled Kevin close, waving a hand to rid Kevin of his clothes as well. He felt his lover awaken and stiffen, then start as he realized he had on no clothing at all.

"Relax, Kevin," he told him softly. "It's just you and me here."

Kevin turned to face him. "What the hell happened? We were talking and then...."

Landon merely looked at him, his glamour down so beautiful blue eyes gazed at him. "You couldn't go with me and you couldn't stop me. It's better if you don't know exactly what happened."

"I'm not stupid. I can figure out what happened. But you somehow forced me to go to sleep. How did you do that?"

Landon raised an eyebrow, amused by the question. "I'm not human, remember? I can do a lot of things. I may be a warrior, but I have other abilities."

"Don't ever do that to me again."

Landon smirked. "I'm not going to promise that. If it's a choice between keeping you safe while pissing you off or you endangering yourself, I'll endure you being pissed at me."

Kevin scowled and looked down at his naked body. "Why are we naked? I'm positive I had clothes on when you left here."

"Yes, you did, but you're not going to need them right now. You're going to give me what we both want because you love me, and patience isn't my virtue."

"So, you're just going to take what you want from me?"

"Nope, you're going to give it to me because you want me too." Landon touched the side of his face affectionately. "I know you and I have issues with each other. I know my actions bother you. I'm not the best at thinking through things, and I may be far older than I look, but age doesn't always equal maturity. So, I know I didn't handle our situation well. But we can't really resist each other, can we?"

Kevin gazed into his eyes. "No, I can't resist you. I love you too much. But how does this work now?"

Landon chuckled. "I'm still the same person. Our sex life doesn't change."

"It is a little different though. You're a lot stronger than you look, and you're this all powerful warrior. Can I really top you?"

Landon grinned. "You're damn right you can and *will*. Being a bottom doesn't make me less of a man or any less dominating. You should know that."

Kevin looked skeptical, and Landon reached down between them, grabbing his erection. Kevin started at the sudden touch but relaxed as Landon began to work him. Kevin closed his eyes, the sensation of Landon's hand moving up and down his shaft always pleasing. He began to move his hips with the motion. Landon knew he wanted more. He lowered his head and took him into his mouth, gaining a moan from Kevin as he slid all the way down his shaft and back up again. Kevin placed his hands on Landon's head as Landon continued the motion, running his fingers through his hair.

Landon worked him with his hand and mouth in combination, driving him into a frenzy. Within a couple of minutes, he felt Kevin pull at his head, trying to signal him to stop. That wasn't on Landon's agenda and he kept going.

"Stop, I can't hold back," Kevin told him breathlessly.

Landon worked him faster, delighting in the gasps that escaped from his lover as he tried to restrain himself. Finally, Kevin couldn't take it anymore. He gripped Landon's head and surged forward deep into his throat, feeling Landon's breath on his balls as he came down his throat. He fell back as the tremors stopped and Landon released him with a grin, though he kept a hand on him.

"We're not done yet."

Kevin looked down at him with an amused look. "What do you plan to do?"

Landon rose over him, straddling his waist and putting his still hard dick at his entrance. Sliding back, he guided Kevin into him, giving a slight hiss at the pain of the intrusion before his body adjusted. Kevin grasped his waist and grabbed two handfuls of ass as Landon began to move, riding him slowly at first. Kevin, still sensitive from coming just moments before, angled his head up and Landon leaned down to capture his lips. Landon's movement was limited, and Kevin began to move instead, surging up into him until Landon moaned against his lips. Kevin wrapped his arms around the other male's waist and began to move faster, his hips like a piston as he bucked up, his sole goal the satisfaction of his partner.

Landon was coasting. He was on the edge of the finale, but not quite there. He opened his eyes when Kevin's hips stopped moving and he felt him beginning to slide off the bed. Kevin hooked his arms under Landon's legs and stood up with him in his arms, still buried deep within him. Landon wrapped his arms around his neck and brought their lips together again as Kevin moved him up and down his shaft. Landon gasped, surprised at the sensation flowing through him. Kevin continued lifting him up and down, each time with more force as he looked to see how much Landon could handle. Their lips separated and Landon buried his face in his neck, muffled sounds escaping him as Kevin worked him up and down his shaft, pushing him ever closer to the climax he was waiting for.

"Come for me," Kevin whispered in his ear.

He continued to lift him up and down with more force, until Landon's muffled sounds of pleasure grew louder. Finally, he threw his head back and cried out as he came over Kevin's stomach. Kevin stopped moving him, letting the aftershocks finish before turning and lowering him to the bed. He kissed him before slowly pulling out and laying down beside him. Sweat covered their bodies and both were a bit out of breath.

"So what happens next?" Kevin asked.

"We continue living our lives," Landon replied. "I'm not going anywhere."

"Good, because I'm not letting you go." Kevin pulled him close to hold him against his chest. "Do you think our troubles are behind us?"

"Now that I have all of my memories, I have to say I honestly don't know. I have a lot of enemies, but I'll do everything I can to keep you safe from that part of my life."

Landon opened his brilliant blue eyes. "As long as you can deal with all that I am, I'll be happy."

"All that you are is all that I need." Kevin looked into his eyes. "I just want to make you happy."

Landon smiled. "You keep the shadows of my past at bay, Kevin. Whatever my future holds, I know you'll be a part of it, and I'm not letting you go either."

Epilogue

M*ay 2011*

It was dinner time at Renee's again and Landon found himself amused at the situation. Kevin and Brian were there, but so was Damien.

"It's been ages since I've had dinner with a group of people I legitimately like," he commented as he sat at the table.

Brian raised an eyebrow. "You know, being royalty really isn't sounding so appealing."

"It's a pain in the ass, which is why I made him king instead of myself," Landon told him as he began bringing in the food to set on the table.

"We hear tales of Avalon all the time but I have to wonder how much is true." Renee followed Landon with more dishes to set out.

"We?" Kevin questioned.

Renee glanced at Landon. "You didn't tell him?"

"It hadn't come up in conversation," Landon replied nonchalantly.

"There's more to the magical circus?" Brian asked.

Renee laughed. "Obviously. I'm a witch but there's far more to it."

Damien chuckled. "Oh yes, the Magi are not the only magical or mystical beings to exist. There's the witches and the vampires too."

"Can't forget the werewolves and demons," Renee added.

"Not to mention the elves and those high strung pricks, the angels," Landon muttered.

"You're fucking with me, aren't you?" Kevin asked.

"Well, Landon is the only one of us that seems to have met an angel but otherwise, no, we're entirely serious," Damien answered honestly.

Kevin blinked several times in surprise. "So, are all those around us?"

"Yeah, there's a few clubs that actually cater to the magical folks but to your eyes, they look no different from any other," Landon explained as he took a seat next to him. "As long as humanity has existed, so have the others."

"Well, some of us predate humans but essentially yes," Damien corrected him.

"You mean, like you personally predate humans or just the race as a whole?" Brian questioned.

"The race as a whole," Damien clarified. "We are long lived with no particular cap on our lives naturally, but the Magi are a constantly warring race. We can die, as can the others."

Kevin sat back to let that settle in his mind, but finally turned to ask Landon a question. "Wait a minute, how old are you really?"

Landon smirked. "I'll be twenty four in October."

Kevin scowled. "You know what I mean."

"That isn't an inaccurate statement," Damien intervened. "When I demanded that he live life as a human, I didn't just strip his powers away. He was reincarnated and born as a mortal. The human mother you met birthed him into the world. However, I take it you want to know the sum total of years he has existed across both lifetimes."

"In that sense, Damien and I are close to the same age. I'm three years older than he is," Landon added.

"That tells me nothing," Kevin grumbled.

Landon grinned at Damien. "You're going to have to tell your age if you want to tell mine, jerk."

Damien managed to look completely unbothered. "All you need to know is that I'm old enough to forget my own age. It doesn't matter at this point."

"So are you old enough to prove or disprove the events in a certain book?" Renee asked.

Landon laughed. "Definitely old enough to disprove a lot of it."

Renee looked to Kevin. "That means over two thousand years old."

"Wouldn't that make them closer to six thousand years old, since two thousand just covers the New Testament?" Brian questioned.

"Holy shit," Kevin muttered.

Landon laughed. "It's better if we don't get anymore specific than that."

"Agreed," Damien added.

Renee and Brian laughed while Kevin just shook his head with a small smile on his face. Clearly, there was a lot more to Landon's life than he'd been told even since finding out he was a Magus.

"So, you can at least dispel some of the myths about the others, right?" Brian asked. "Like the whole turning others into vampires and werewolves."

"Both are possible." Landon started fixing his own plate. "We're immune. The blood lines don't mix, so I can't be turned into a vampire or a werewolf. The bites hurt like a bitch though."

"See, now there's a story I've never heard and definitely need to know," Renee pointed out while also beginning to prepare her own plate.

"There's a lot of those to tell," Damien pointed out, joining in with fixing himself food. "Landon and I have had a lot of time to get involved with things everywhere. Before I was king, we came into the mortal world often."

Landon snorted. "We came here just as often after I secured your throne. While we may have our own realm, there's no avoiding being involved with the affairs of the other races for the most part. Most Magi avoid the demons and angels are preachy little fuckers that only deal with a select few. Normally to meddle in shit they should leave alone."

"I'm disappointed I didn't get to meet any of the angels," Damien pouted.

"Give it time, they'll come around. They pestered me enough," Landon assured him.

"You're so nonchalant about all this," Kevin commented.

Landon shrugged. "If any one of those fuckers can actually kill me, the world is probably screwed. Why stress over it?"

"There are laws to limit the actions of us all," Damien assured Kevin. "But it's safe to say that the majority of people you might come across will give you a wide berth because of your boyfriend here."

Brian had already gone through his first plate of food and was on his second. "There's no point in worrying about it. They've been around all this time and haven't done anything to you."

DRAKO

"I'll teach you how to spot them later, just to make you feel better," Landon promised.

"I can learn to do that?" Kevin asked.

"You should be able to as long as you pay attention," Landon answered.

"Speaking of teaching, I have a proposition for you," Damien interjected.

Landon raised an eyebrow. "I'm already teaching your kid. What more do you want?"

"Well, I remember a hobby of yours and an opportunity has presented itself here. How do you feel about running a school?" Damien's grin didn't make Landon feel any easier about the proposition.

"Are you serious?" Landon questioned.

"Most definitely. It'll let you get out of that job you have now and work at your leisure. I figured it'd be easier if you ran your own business now and why not do something you enjoy?"

Landon sighed. "This is an order disguised as a proposition, isn't it?"

Damien grinned. "It's a proposition, one that I would personally appreciate you at least giving real consideration to. It's about time you show Kevin you have talents other than the ones he knows about, don't you think?"

Landon rolled his eyes. "Fine, I'll do it. I know what you're getting at already."

"Excellent, we can go see it when we're done here tonight."

Landon shook his head as Kevin looked at him with a raised eyebrow. "I'm sure there's more to it but I happen to sing and dance. They tell me I have a decent voice and dancing isn't too different from fighting if you work at it."

212

"Oh, *this* we have to go along for." Renee grinned. "You never sing around other people."

"Naturally it has another purpose to it but for the sake of blending in, it'll be a dance school," Damien told them. "I figured you'd want to decorate and set up personally."

"Definitely," Landon agreed. "I can't wait to get started."

Don't miss out!

Visit the website below and you can sign up to receive emails whenever Drako publishes a new book. There's no charge and no obligation.

https://books2read.com/r/B-A-TPBDB-UDPDD

Connecting independent readers to independent writers.

Also by Drako

Journeys
Shadows of the Past

The Coven
Bewitched Souls (The Coven #1)
Sunder (The Coven #2)

The Dragon Hunters
The Lost Dragon (The Dragon Hunters #1)
The Dragon Witch (The Dragon Hunters #2)
Fatal Healing (The Dragon Hunters #3)
Heir of Mjölnir (The Dragon Hunters #4)
Relinquished Mercy (The Dragon Hunters #5)
Blood Monarch (The Dragon Hunters #6)

Watch for more at www.drakosden.com.

About the Author

Drako was born in 1987 in St. Louis, Missouri. He is mainly a fantasy writer, though he also writes some poetry and general fiction. He is very active on both twitter and facebook and has his own website at www.drakosden.com which is frequently updated with news on his books and fun extras. When he isn';t writing, he's busy helping take care of his nieces and sons, playing videogames, reading, promoting, and spending time with family. He also just recently started a podcast at https://anchor.fm/drako5 which goes to several other platforms, including spotify, google podcasts, and apple

Read more at www.drakosden.com.

Milton Keynes UK
Ingram Content Group UK Ltd.
UKHW020730130524
442628UK00001B/24